Dragonology Chronicles

Keep reading!
Keep going!
@HiddenGemsLiterary
Emporium

Dragonology Chronicles

VOLUME ONE

THE DRAGON'S EYE

Dugald A. Steer

illustrated by Douglas Carrel

CANDLEWICK PRESS
CAMBRIDGE, MASSACHUSETTS

Text copyright © 2006 by Dugald A. Steer
Illustrations copyright © 2006 by Douglas Carrel

First edition 2006

Library of Congress Cataloging-in-Publication Data is available.

Library of Congress Catalog Card Number pending

ISBN 978-0-7636-2810-9

2 4 6 8 10 9 7 5 3

Printed in the United States of America

This book was typeset in Granjon.

Candlewick Press
2067 Massachusetts Avenue
Cambridge, Massachusetts 02140

visit us at www.candlewick.com

A NOTE TO THE READER

This map of the British Isles shows some of the locations visited by Dr. Ernest Drake and his two dragonological apprentices Daniel and Beatrice Cook during the course of this adventure. Apart from the locations of the lairs of those dragons that are visited during the story, and which must perforce be revealed, it does not indicate any other sites where dragons may be found; this has been done in order to minimise contact between these creatures and humans who have not undergone training by the Secret and Ancient Society of Dragonologists.

Should any reader discover evidence of a dragon's lair or any other signs of dragon activity, it is requested that they take great care and investigate further only with the help of one of Dr. Drake's books on the subject.

The British Isles

PROLOGUE

At quarter past six on the morning of Friday July 7, 1882, a black carriage burst out of the entrance of Tottenham Court Road in London so quickly that it had to veer to avoid a bird fancier's cart that was coming down Oxford Street. The carriage—which was of the old-fashioned type known as a brougham—tipped onto one of its wheels, and for a moment seemed as though it was going to fall onto its side before the driver managed to right it and sped off towards St. Giles. As the carriage thundered by, the exotic birds sent up such a terrible cackling and squawking that the cart driver had to stop to pull a tarpaulin over the cages.

The carriage continued down St. Andrew's Street and into Wyvern Way. At the sound of a sharp tapping from inside, the driver of the brougham halted the vehicle and the top of an ornate dragon-headed black cane jabbed out towards a rather curious little shop that, judging by the display in its ancient windows, might easily have been the very shop where the cane itself had been purchased.

The driver and his mate went round to the back of the carriage and untied the large wooden crate that was lashed to the back. As it was still early, they were observed by no one, except for a stray dog that had been nosing through a pile of rubbish and that now came sniffing round the wheels of the carriage. But as soon as it put up its nose to sniff the crate, it froze, its wispy hair standing on end and its ears shaking, before it leapt away, yelping in terror. The driver grunted and was just about to lift off the crate when it shook so violently that he was almost knocked off his feet. He then stood looking at the crate until the dragon-headed cane jabbed out of the carriage once more and gave him a nasty poke. A thin voice hissed, "For goodness' sakes, get on with it!"

The driver nodded to his mate, and the pair of them lifted the crate off the back of the carriage and shuffled it over to the doorway of the shop. The driver returned to his seat and picked up his whip, while the other man went up to the shop and rang the bell as loudly as he could several times, before climbing back onto the carriage himself. Only when the driver was certain that he could hear noises coming from one of the little rooms above the shop did he crack his whip and send the carriage speeding off down the narrow street and into St. Martin's Lane. A man of about sixty with a large walrus moustache and an old-fashioned nightcap opened one of the windows and put his head out, just catching sight of the rear end of the carriage rounding the corner. The man looked at where it had disappeared for a moment and then, hearing thumping noises from the street below, looked down to see the crate that had been left so unceremoniously on his doorstep. It was shaking violently, and thin jets of smoke issued from several holes in one of its sides.

Meanwhile, the black brougham set off into Whitehall and turned into a street of government buildings, stopping in front of a black door. A tall man whose features were mostly hidden by a high-collared coat and a top hat climbed out of the carriage and, after checking that there was no one about, rapped on the door with a dragon-headed cane.

When there was no answer, he rapped again, more loudly. There was still no answer, so he rapped a third time, at which a butler finally opened the door and, raising his eyebrows at the appearance of the visitor, said, "Yes?"

"I come in the name of Ebenezer Crook," hissed the man. "My mission is urgent. I must speak to your master immediately."

"I am afraid the Minister is in bed," said the butler.

"This is an emergency," said the man. "Please inform him right away."

"Inform him of what?"

"Ah," said the man, twisting his cane irritably. "I fear I must tell him that myself. Mention Mr. Crook's name to him the minute he wakes; I'm sure he will see me right away."

The butler shook his head, then disappeared inside.

He quickly returned.

"The Minister will see you at once, sir," he said.

As he ushered the man into the building, the butler glanced over at the brougham. Inside, looking out at him with two jet-black eyes, her pale white face framed by black hair, sat the most beautiful woman he had ever seen.

CHAPTER ONE
WYVERN WAY

The scientific study of dragons requires
intelligence and courage above all else, as young
dragonologists find out soon enough.
—— Dr. Drake's Dragon Diary, January 1842

In July of 1882, I was twelve years old and had never heard of Dr. Ernest Drake. I had certainly never met a dragon. In fact, the whole idea of fire-breathing, scaly monsters that could blast me with flame or tear me limb from limb couldn't have been further from my mind as I rode on a train through London. I was on my way to Waterloo Station to meet my parents. They were returning from India to spend the summer holidays with my sister, Beatrice, and me. I hadn't seen them in four years, and I was thinking about their last visit. I remembered how excited I had felt as they came striding down the gangplank of their ship wearing big smiles, bringing us presents, and talking of mountains and maharajas and elephant rides into the jungle. I was sure this summer was going to be even better. Four years is a long time to wait before seeing your parents, but now the waiting was over.

The train pulled into Waterloo. Beatrice was already there. She was standing by her suitcase, her long brown hair tied with a ribbon under her straw hat. But she was holding a letter and biting her lip.

"Hello, Daniel," she said, giving me a weak smile.

"What's in the letter?" I asked.

Beatrice looked at the floor while she handed it to me. It was in my mother's handwriting.

"It arrived this morning," she said.

I took it and read:

My Dearest Beatrice and Daniel,

I hope this letter finds you both well. As you know, Father and I had such high hopes of being able to return to see you this summer. But something terribly important has come up, and the Prince of Jaisalmer—the Maharawal himself—has made an urgent request for us to stay. You will know how important it is because we love you both so dearly and I feel desperate that I will miss another summer of your growing up.

Your father suggested that you might like to stay with Uncle Algernon, but we have talked things over and decided that it is time for you to get to know our old friend Dr. Ernest Drake. He has a house in Sussex and a little shop in London that he keeps as a sort of hobby. I have asked him to meet you at Waterloo if he can. If for any reason he is not there to meet you, you can find his shop quite easily by going to Trafalgar Square and walking up St. Martin's Lane until you see a street called Wyvern Way. You can't miss the shop because there is a large sign with his name on it hanging above the door.

I must go now because they have asked us to go and see the Maharawal at once.

With our dearest, fondest wishes,
Mother

By the time I finished the letter, I felt my face burning. I handed it back to Beatrice, who was still looking at the floor, making little fists with her hands. This was the second summer that our parents had failed to meet us on short notice. The year before, there had been another mysterious emergency that had seen us packed off to Uncle Algernon's. Life there had been so monotonous that I had been almost glad to get back to boarding school.

"Who's Dr. Drake?" I asked.

"Don't you remember him?" said Beatrice. "He came to visit us when Father was ill. He has an enormous moustache that gets soup in it. All he ever talks about is dragons. Uncle Algernon told me that he has dangerous ideas and that we shouldn't listen to people like him if we want to grow up to be intelligent members of society."

I didn't remember clearly. I had a vague impression of a jolly man with a big moustache coming to stay with us when I was five. I remembered pretending to be an iguanodon and chasing him round the garden while he laughed. But I had no idea his name was Drake.

"Is he a real doctor?" I asked.

"No," said Beatrice. "I think he's a dracocologist or something. But I'm sure he got Father the job in India. I hate him."

"At least he sounds better than Uncle Algernon," I said.

We looked round the station. There were a lot of porters carrying luggage and people hurrying to catch trains, but no men with enormous moustaches, apart from a couple of guards.

"You see," said Beatrice after we had been waiting for an hour. "He hasn't even bothered to turn up and meet us. I expect he's too busy with his dragons."

"Does he really know about them?" I asked.

Beatrice laughed. "No one really knows about dragons, Daniel. They don't exist."

When we left Waterloo Station, it was drizzling, but it didn't take us long to reach the river and cross over towards Trafalgar Square. We found St. Martin's Lane and walked up past the church towards the axis of old streets that is called the Seven Dials. Our surroundings grew shabbier the farther we went. In Trafalgar Square everyone had been bustling about on some important business, but here people seemed to have nothing to do but loiter about. Even though it was raining, they stood propped against lampposts or lurked in the doorways of the pubs with dark, dirty windows that lined the street on either side. In between the pubs were pawnbroker's shops, dingy grocer's shops and eateries, and in between those quite a few bird and rabbit fancier's shops.

"Are you sure we're going the right way?" whispered Beatrice, walking so closely beside me that our suitcases bumped together.

"The sign definitely said St. Martin's Lane," I said.

"Well, it's a funny place for a shop if you ask me," said Beatrice.

Suddenly, a woman in a tattered dress lunged towards us from one of the pub doorways. She was holding out a bunch of heather.

"Buy some lucky heather, my love?" said the woman as she reached over to place a bunch in Beatrice's pocket. Beatrice managed to dodge her, then stiffened and walked on. But the woman stepped round in front of us, barring our way.

"You're a pretty thing," she said, this time placing the heather in the band of Beatrice's straw hat with a skilled hand.

At that, Beatrice stepped in front of me, looked the woman in the eye, and said, "I don't want any heather, thank you."

Then she took the heather out of her hat and held it out to the woman, who withdrew her hand immediately. Beatrice let the heather fall to the ground and grabbed my arm.

"Come on," she said, and we began walking away at a half trot.

"You'll pay for that!" the woman called after us.

I looked back, emboldened by my sister's courage.

"We haven't got any money," I said.

"We'll see about that!" shouted the woman. She turned to a group of rough-looking boys of about our age, who had been playing marbles but who were now standing watching us.

"Vincent! Michael! Oliver! There's a thief for you! She says she hasn't got any money. If it's true, there'll be a shilling for you if you can take that hat from her and give that brat with her a nice shiner."

At that, both Beatrice and I started running. But the three boys, who weren't carrying luggage, as we were, quickly caught up with us and surrounded us in a shop doorway. Beatrice stood in front of me again and looked at them defiantly. Across the damp street, in the doorway of yet another pub, I noticed a well-dressed man watching us with some interest. He had a top hat, his collar was pulled up high, and he was carrying some sort of cane with a strangely carved top.

"Help us!" Beatrice cried to him.

But instead of helping, the man simply ducked back farther into the shadow of the doorway.

"He's got to have his shiner," said the largest boy, rolling up his right shirtsleeve and pointing at me.

"Come and give it to him then," said Beatrice, standing aside a little.

I was horrified.

But as soon as the boy reached in to grab me, Beatrice got hold of his ear and gave it a tug so hard that he yelped. I was amazed. It seemed to knock all of the stuffing out of him at once.

"Go away," said Beatrice.

"Ow!" he howled. "All right. We were only messing about. I wasn't really going to hit him. It was a joke. Let me go!"

Beatrice let him go with a shove, then turned to the other boys.

"Are you going to give my brother a shiner?"

But the other boys were disappearing up the road as fast as they could. My sister really is quite remarkable at times.

I suddenly remembered the mysterious man. I looked over at the pub doorway, but he was gone. Then we turned round to look at the shop whose doorway we were standing in. In some ways it was quite like the rest of the small, dingy shops that lined the street, except for one important difference—its bottle-green windows were completely full of the most amazing array of statues and carvings of dragons that I had ever seen. And over the top of the shop window was a large sign that read

Doctor Drake's Dragonalia

"Ugh!" said Beatrice. "Dragons!"

CHAPTER TWO
DR. DRAKE'S DRAGONALIA

To the experienced eye, it is easy to tell at once when
a dragon's range has been entered, as well as exactly
what type of dragon is being encountered.
—— DR. DRAKE'S DRAGON DIARY, MAY 1842

There was no bell, but the door to Dr. Drake's Dragonalia was open, so I turned the handle and went in. I
looked around and gasped. The shop was full of shelves
stacked high with old books, vases, walking sticks, statues,
games, and candlesticks, and every single one was decorated
with pictures of dragons: dragons sleeping, dragons roaring,
dragons breathing fire, and dragons carrying off elephants
or fighting Saint George. But there was no sign of Dr.
Drake himself.

"Oh, dear. He's worse than I thought," said Beatrice.

Her brow wrinkled in a frown.

"I wonder if that's why Dr. Drake wanted our parents to
go to India," she said.

"Why?" I asked.

"To send him things like this," she said, pointing to a small Indian statue of a snake with a man's head coiled round a rock, with a little label that said, NAGA [JAIPUR, 1850] 10/6.

At the back of the room was a counter with a bell, and behind that was a half-open door through which I could see a staircase going down. As I drew near to the counter, I could hear distant voices coming up the stairs. One of them was shouting. I hoped that Dr. Drake wasn't going to turn out to be one of those adults who are always angry. Since someone was sure to come up soon, I decided to content myself with taking a closer look at the things on the shelves. But Beatrice went straight round behind the counter, put her head through the door, and cried out, "Shop!"

At that, we heard a loud clatter coming from below, which, added to shouting, was rather alarming.

"Do you think we ought to find a policeman?" I asked. "In case there's something wrong?"

"What, and nearly have my hat stolen again?" said Beatrice. "Anyway, lots of adults shout all the time. There's probably nothing wrong at all."

"Then let's go downstairs and see if we can find someone who knows Dr. Drake," I said.

"All right," agreed Beatrice.

But we were only halfway down the stairs when I heard a horrible roaring screech coming from behind one of the doors in the lower hallway. A young man in a chequered waistcoat and shirtsleeves burst out of it, followed by a large cloud of smoke. He slammed the door firmly behind him, ran towards the end of the corridor, opened another door, and disappeared inside.

The cloud of smoke in the hall soon vanished, leaving a strange, sulphurous odour, and we were left alone again, standing on the stairs. It was Beatrice who spoke first.

"Let's wait upstairs," she whispered.

"But we have to find Dr. Drake," I whispered back.

I took a step down, while Beatrice took one up, glaring at me. I had become terribly curious about whatever roaring, screeching creature had caused the smoke. Surely it could not have been what I hoped—and feared at the same time— it might be? I took another step down.

"Daniel!" whispered Beatrice as loudly as she dared. "Come up here and wait!"

"I'll only be a minute," I whispered.

"Hmmph!" hissed Beatrice, pointing back up towards the open door. "Hmmmmph!"

I ignored her. Looking very red-faced, she turned and clattered back up towards the shop as noisily as she possibly could and rang the bell on the counter two or three times, crying, "Shop!" each time she did so.

"Shop! Shop!"

At first I froze, but no one seemed to notice Beatrice's shouting. So I continued down into the corridor and quietly approached the door. I was just about to bend down and look through the keyhole when the shouting started again at the opposite end of the corridor. I could only hear one side of the conversation, because the replies were uttered so softly, I could make nothing of them. This is what I heard:

"What if it gets loose? Have you thought of that?"

"You do understand the danger, I take it?"

"Never mind who reported it!"

"But it's right here in London!"

"You are quite sure that *you* have not been hypnotised?"

"I can only hope that the Minister's trust in you has not been misplaced, Doctor."

And, "Believe me, if you do not, there will be the most dire consequences."

The conversation continued, but by now I was even more anxious to see what might be in the room where the smoke had come from. So I turned towards the door again and put my eye to the keyhole. Everything seemed dark inside at first, but as my eyes adjusted, I was able to make out what lay beyond. The room, which was lit by two candles, was in a terrible state of disarray. Many of the books from the bookshelves that lined the walls had been knocked onto the floor. There were three desks piled high with bottles of liquids, oddly shaped specimen jars, and a multitude of other strange objects. At least two of the desks looked as though they had been ransacked, and one jar had been smashed, its contents gently fizzing into the stone floor. The same sweet, sulphurous odour that I had smelt in the corridor was coming from the keyhole. Suddenly I saw a smallish creature spring out from behind one of the desks and dash round the room, half leaping and half flying. Was it some kind of large bird, after all? I decided to open the door just a little to see it more clearly. I gently began to turn the handle. Almost at once, I heard the bell ring again and Beatrice's shrill voice calling out, "Shop! Shop!"

I'll "Shop" you! I thought. As I turned the handle, the bird—or whatever it was—grew perfectly quiet. So I was very, very careful indeed as I edged the door open little by little.

BOOM! Something smashed into the door with such force that it knocked me over backwards. Something that I still could hardly make out was flying round and round the room. I could see wings, scales, and a wisp of smoke rising from its nostrils. I saw it fly over to the other side of the room, positioning itself directly opposite me. With wings outspread and claws at the ready, it fixed me with its beady eyes and began to fly straight at me.

BANG! Someone came up behind me and slammed the door shut. I looked up to see an old gentleman with a large moustache, leaning over me in a very disapproving manner, holding the door shut with one hand, and wagging his finger at me with the other.

"Daniel Cook, I presume?" he said.

CHAPTER THREE
THE NATURAL HISTORIAN

Curiosity may not actually have killed the cat, but it has certainly caused the untimely demise of many a promising dragonologist.

—— DR. DRAKE'S DRAGON DIARY, MAY 1842

D o you make a habit of spying through keyholes, Daniel?" asked Dr. Drake, after he had introduced himself.

"No, sir," I said. "I was looking for you and I heard shouting and a lot of banging about. I only looked through the keyhole to see what was making the commotion."

"And after you'd looked through the keyhole, you decided to open the door and have a better look, did you?"

"Er, yes, sir," I stammered.

"Did your sister, Beatrice, have a look, too?"

"No, sir," I said. "She waited upstairs."

"Good," said Dr. Drake.

Just then the door at the end of the corridor opened, and a

short man with a red face and a dark suit emerged. He took out his watch and pointed to it meaningfully.

Dr. Drake leaned towards me and said, "Then you may wait upstairs, Daniel. You may look at the things in my shop, but don't touch them. And remember, not a word of what you have seen—or *think* you have seen—to anyone. Understand?"

"Yes, sir," I said.

When I was halfway up the stairs, I turned back to look at Dr. Drake. He put a finger to his lips and said sternly, "Not . . . a . . . word!"

"What happened?" asked Beatrice when I had arrived back at the counter. "He caught you snooping and gave you a good telling off, by the sounds of it!"

"Nothing happened," I replied. "But he doesn't seem as nice as I thought he was going to be. I think he's going to turn out to be one of those cross people. He says we are to wait for him."

Downstairs, the shouting had started again. Then I heard two loud bangs as if the creature—whatever it was—was trying to smash the door down.

"What on earth *is* that?" said Beatrice.

I didn't speak for a moment. Dr. Drake had told me not to say anything, but Beatrice *was* my sister. Didn't I have a duty to warn her?

I summoned up my courage and said, "Don't tell Dr.

Drake I told you this, but there's something you should know. He's got a dragon down there."

"A dragon, Daniel?" scoffed Beatrice in the patronising I'm-a-year-older-than-you voice that I always hated. "Don't be silly. There are no such things as dragons."

"And I'm telling you it *was* a dragon!" I said. "It had scales and claws and everything. The room was full of smoke!"

Beatrice thought for a moment. There were three more loud bangs. Then she grinned.

"Ugh," she said. "I've just had a horrible idea."

"Yes?" I asked.

"What if Dr. Drake is a mad scientist? What if he collects lizards and birds and then . . . cuts them up . . . and does horrible things to them?"

"Like Dr. Frankenstein?" I said, laughing.

"Yes, but with lizards and birds," she said.

"That doesn't seem very likely," I said, shuddering despite myself.

"Well, excuse me, Daniel, but the idea that he has a real dragon down there doesn't seem very likely to me, either."

I didn't have much to say to that. Beatrice was obviously going to have to see the dragon before she believed in it, so I went back to looking round the shop. Behind the counter, there were some old paintings and a couple of drawings leaning against the wall. As I flicked through them, I could see that they were mostly of dragons, as I had expected. Beatrice came and looked at them over my shoulder.

"They're pastiches," she said.

"What's a pastiche?" I asked.

"When we were at Uncle Algernon's, Cousin Jocasta and I managed to borrow a book on the history of art. It had a lot of colour plates in it. This one looks like one of those Italian painters—Leonardo da something," she said. "And this one looks like a German artist who did a famous drawing of a rabbit, only this is a dragon in the same pose. And this one looks like Turner, who liked to do stormy skies."

"It looks like a mess," I said.

"But can't you see?" said Beatrice. "Instead of the original paintings, these ones are all copies, only they have pictures of dragons in them."

Then she let out a gasp. For the next picture didn't have any dragons in it. Instead, it was a simple watercolour of a group of people standing in front of a small hill. And there, standing right next to Dr. Drake, were two people who could only have been our mother and father.

"I knew it," said Beatrice bitterly. "He sent them away. I hate him."

But then I pointed out someone else in the picture, over on the other side. It was a younger version of the same man who had been watching us from the doorway of the pub that very morning. Even in the picture, there was something creepy about him. I turned the picture over and looked at the back of it, to see if it said anything about where it had been painted. In faint red pencil, I could just make out the words:

S.A.S.D. Picnic, Silbury Hill, Somerset, June 1868

I quickly started flicking through the stack of paintings to see if there were any more like that. Then a door slammed in the corridor, and I heard the sound of someone coming up the stairs.

It was the young man who I'd seen fleeing across the corridor earlier. He was carrying a brown paper bag in one hand and, in the other, a jug and two glasses.

"Hey!" he said, giving us an enormous smile. He spoke with an American accent. "Would I be having the pleasure of addressing Master Daniel and Miss Beatrice Cook?" he asked.

Beatrice, who never trusts anyone until she knows something about him or her, did not smile back.

"Yes, that's right," she said. "And who are you?"

"You can call me Emery," he said. "Emery Cloth. Dr. Drake said you might be hungry, so I've brought you a little something to eat."

He offered the paper bag to us and placed the jug down on the counter with the glasses.

"We're not hungry," said Beatrice.

"Then that's too bad," said Emery, giving me a wink. "But I'll leave these here anyway."

Emery went back downstairs.

I looked in the paper bag, which contained cucumber sandwiches, and looked in the jug, which contained water.

"What do you mean, 'We're not hungry'?" I said.

"Daniel, I don't know if we can trust Dr. Drake," she said. "I don't know if we should stay here."

"Why?" I asked.

"Look what happened to our parents," she said.

"As far as we know, nothing has happened to them," I said.

"All right," said Beatrice. "Then since our parents wrote to us about him, I'll trust him until I find out—one way or the other."

And she grabbed a sandwich and began to devour it ravenously.

Chapter Four
ST. LEONARD'S FOREST

*I often think back to my childhood. I was a lucky
boy——I grew up with my very own dragon living in
the woods at the bottom of my garden.*
—— Dr. Drake's Dragon Diary, June 1842

Waiting for three hours in Dr. Drake's Dragonalia while trying not to touch anything was like being a starving man in a roomful of food he was not allowed to eat. I was desperate to ask someone about the dragon I had seen, and I was in a shop full of some of the most interesting objects I had ever come across. Finally, at five o'clock, the short red-faced man who I had seen earlier came thumping up the stairs, looking even more red-faced than before, and dashed out of the shop. Then, Dr. Drake emerged. As he stood before us, his eyes caught sight of the stack of paintings and his face broke into a wide smile.

"Good afternoon, Beatrice," he said. And then, turning to me, he continued, "And Daniel. I see that you have been admiring my paintings. I am collecting them for a book. I have many artist friends who are very helpful to me at times. I'm sorry that I couldn't come to meet you both, but as you see, something important has come up and I have had to attend to it."

Beatrice glanced at me. I knew that she was thinking that our parents had said more or less exactly the same thing.

"But never mind," said Dr. Drake. "I was sure that such clever children as yourselves would have no problems finding my little shop. When I sent Emery to make sure that you were safe, I asked him to watch you closely and see how you did. You both handled yourselves excellently. I don't think Daniel would have looked quite so handsome with a black eye."

"Who was that other man?" I asked.

"What other man?" said Dr. Drake.

"There was a man standing over there," I said, gesturing out of the window at the pub doorway on the other side of the street. "He had a strangely carved cane and he looked creepy. He's in that picture along with you and our parents."

Dr. Drake looked at the picture. Although he did his best to hide it, I could see him give a slight shudder.

"Ah!" he exclaimed. "That is Ignatius Crook. I have not seen him for a long time. Perhaps he wanted to visit me but changed his mind when he saw that I already had visitors."

"And what about the drag—" I began, but Dr. Drake interrupted me.

"Now, Daniel," he said, "since you are both coming to stay with me in St. Leonard's Forest and I am to find lovely things for you to do, we had better set off right away. We have a long journey ahead of us tonight."

Many hours later, I awoke with a jolt when the carriage hit a small pothole. The rain that had been falling all day in London had given way to a clear, moonlit sky in Sussex, and I could see that we were passing through a dense forest full of many different kinds of trees.

"Nearly there!" cried Dr. Drake cheerfully, pointing out of the window to the pale circle of light cast by the dull beam of the carriage's lanterns. "Can you see them?"

I moved over to the window and peered out with great interest. I had fallen asleep thinking about dragons and dragon-hunting expeditions and deciding that I couldn't really see how they could be mythological at all. Was Dr. Drake actually pointing out a dragon to me now? As I peered out of the window, I spotted several small shapes moving—or rather, hopping and scampering—along the road before us and in the grass verge that ran along the side. The carriage veered slightly to avoid one of them, and suddenly I realised what they were.

"Rabbits!" I said. There were hundreds of them.

"Indeed," said Dr. Drake. "St. Leonard's Forest is home to one of the largest warrens in England. They make quite a mess of my garden, as you will see, but in the forest I always feel that it is I who am the interloper, and so I do little about it. But we are arriving at my home. Welcome to Castle Drake!"

As the carriage turned off the main road and began going down a long drive, I saw that we had reached a rather ramshackle old house, surrounded by an old, crumbling wall and a number of outbuildings. I could see what Dr. Drake meant about the rabbits. His lawn was quite pockmarked.

Several rabbits hopped away among the trees as we stepped, yawning sleepily, from the carriage.

The coachman brought down our luggage.

"Many thanks," said Dr. Drake. "If you follow the road round and take the first lane on the left, you will find the inn I spoke about. The landlord will be expecting you."

"What is the name of the inn?" asked the coachman.

"Why," said Dr. Drake with a grin, "it is called the Dragon." And so saying, he turned, drew out a large key, and unlocked his front door. Once inside, he lit a candle for each of us and led us upstairs, where he showed us into two rooms that lay at the end of a long corridor. My own room, which seemed quite a little dormitory, had four beds in it, but I did not see how many were in Beatrice's.

"It is lucky that I am in the habit of keeping rooms for strangers," said Dr. Drake. "Although I do not think we will be strangers for long! Good night!" And with that he left us.

I put down my small suitcase and sat down on one of the beds. I thought about the strange experience I had had in Dr. Drake's shop. I also realised that, whoever he was, Dr. Drake was certainly *not* one of those adults who are cross all the time.

CHAPTER FIVE
CASTLE DRAKE

Dreaming of dragons usually means one of two
things: there are dragons nearby, or you had too much
supper the night before.

—— Dr. Drake's Dragon Diary, October 1842

My first night at Castle Drake was a restless one. I dreamt that I rode in a carriage, driven, I supposed in my dream, by Dr. Drake. It hurtled down dark, starlit lanes through an inky-black forest where dragons lurked. Whenever I went to look outside to see if I could find out what had happened to Beatrice, a large leathery creature with piercing eyes and sharp claws bashed into the carriage windows with such force that I was sure they were going to break.

When I woke, I got up at once, dressed hurriedly, and went downstairs into the hall. I was disappointed that the house showed no signs of belonging to the owner of the magnificent Dr. Drake's Dragonalia. It seemed like a very ordinary house indeed. Smells of bacon led me to the kitchen, where I was surprised to find Beatrice already tucking in to a large breakfast. A short lady in a brown dress and spectacles was bending over to stir some mushrooms on the stove.

The woman smiled when she saw me.

"*Bonjour,*" she said. "I am Dr. Drake's housekeeper. My name is Mademoiselle Gamay. I am pleased to meet you. I hope you slept well?"

I glanced over at Beatrice. I didn't think that either of us had slept particularly well, but I looked at Mademoiselle Gamay and said, "Very well, thank you."

"*S'il vous plaît!* Sit down and have a cup of tea and some breakfast," said Mademoiselle Gamay. "It is doctor's orders, you know."

And so I sat down. But as soon as Mademoiselle Gamay had put a cup of tea and a plate of food in front of me, she looked at me over the top of her spectacles, laughed, and said, "Do you know? Your sister told me she slept well, too. You will be the first children I have known that slept well on their first night in *this* house!"

Beatrice and I looked at each other. Whatever could she mean? There was silence for a moment, and then Beatrice looked up and asked, "Do lots of children come here, then?"

"Only a few lucky ones," said Mademoiselle Gamay with a smile. "But surely you know why you're here?"

"We were supposed to meet our parents, but they couldn't come, so they sent us to stay with Dr. Drake," said Beatrice.

"Did you visit Dr. Drake's shop?" asked Mademoiselle Gamay.

"Yes," answered Beatrice.

"Did you see downstairs?"

"Ye—" I began.

"No," answered Beatrice.

"Not really," I agreed.

"Did you meet Emery?"

"Yes," said Beatrice.

"And you don't know why you're here?"

"To learn all about drag—?" I began.

"To stay with Dr. Drake," said Beatrice, interrupting me.

"Well," said Mademoiselle Gamay, "I won't tell you any more. I don't want to spoil the surprise. Have some more tea, eat your breakfast, and then wait for Dr. Drake in the drawing room. I am sure that he will explain everything."

The drawing room was small and neat, with a window that faced the front lawn. Three rabbits were hopping about lazily down at the far end. The only interesting thing in the room was a small bookshelf in the corner, and I went straight over to it. But instead of the fascinating volumes about dragons, wizards, pirates, or ancient Egypt that I had hoped to find, there was a series of dull-looking tomes about geography, politics, natural history, economic theory, and one particularly uninviting-looking volume entitled *The History of Benzene in the Manufacturing Industries.*

"Good morning," said Dr. Drake when he arrived.

"Mademoiselle Gamay tells me that you hardly got a wink of sleep last night. Well, well. I am sorry, but I am not surprised. Now as I have told you, something important has come up, and I will be very busy. But it will not be long before the other children arrive and our summer school begins."

"*Summer* school?" said Beatrice. She sounded as though it was almost too good to be true. *If only she knew what* real *learning was like,* I thought.

"Yes," said Dr. Drake, smiling. "That is one of the reasons your parents sent you to me."

"But what will we learn?" I asked.

"What would you like to learn?" he said.

"About drag—" I began. But Beatrice interrupted me again.

"About science and literature and art and languages and chemistry and mathematics," she said.

"Excellent!" said Dr. Drake. "Then it looks as though we will have our work cut out for us. But I'm afraid school does not start for a week. Until then, you must sometimes amuse yourselves. Without looking into any places that you shouldn't, please," he added, looking at me.

"Of course not," I said.

"Today," continued Dr. Drake, "I must take a walk into the forest to collect various plants and other things that I need. Beatrice, I would be delighted if you would accompany me. I think that you will enjoy learning about some of the beautiful flora and fauna we have out here in the country-side. Daniel, I rather fear I will not invite you along on our little expedition. You shall stay here. I do not think we need discuss the reason why?"

I knew very well why. It was a punishment for my key-hole spying the day before. I nodded glumly and looked out the window. There were suddenly only two rabbits on the lawn.

"Very good," said Dr. Drake. "Then I advise you to spend the day broadening your education. I think you know enough Latin verbs to get started with. There are plenty of books here, as you can see, which should suffice to entertain you. But you must remember not to go looking into rooms and places that do not concern you. Mademoiselle Gamay will come back to the house at around half past twelve to give you some lunch."

And without further ado, Dr. Drake collected a large leather bag and a stick from the hall, opened the front door, and set off with long strides down a path that led off from the main driveway towards the forest, accompanied by my sister, who, to my surprise, followed him without a word.

CHAPTER SIX

ON THE ORIGIN OF SPECIES

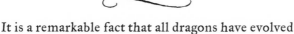

It is a remarkable fact that all dragons have evolved
to suit the habitats in which they live.
—— DR. DRAKE'S DRAGON DIARY, MAY 1842

W hen Beatrice and Dr. Drake had gone, I decided that
I might as well try to find a book to read. I love natural history—the animals, birds, and fishes of the world
have always fascinated me—and when I saw a volume by a
man I had heard of, Charles Darwin, I thought that I might
as well give it a try. So I picked it up, opened it, and began to
read:

When on board H.M.S. *Beagle* as naturalist, I was much
struck with certain facts in the distribution of the inhabitants of South America, and in the geological relations
of the present to the past inhabitants of that continent.

It was not the easiest of books, but I found that it did get a little more straightforward after a while, and I did manage to get some idea of what Darwin was writing about. But what really interested me I found on the fifth or sixth page. At the bottom were three perfect sketches of dragon's heads. At least the one on the right looked like a proper dragon's head. The one on the left looked more like it had come from a dinosaur, while the middle one seemed to be something in between. And under the picture was a handwritten note that said, *As the dragon's head evolved, so also did the fangs and venom-producing organs responsible for the remarkable phenomenon of fire breathing.*

At that, I began to flick through the book, finding several sketches of dragons that seemed to be illustrating points Darwin was making. There was a series of claw sketches and a sketch showing what it called "wing development." Another set of sketches seemed to show how a baby dragon developed in its egg. And a later sketch showed a duck-billed platypus with the caption *Some believed that the original specimen was a stitched-together fake.* I decided that when I grew up, I didn't just want to be any old explorer but a dragon explorer. Soon I was imagining going to India to trek through the jungle to search for dragons in lost caves.

When it was time for lunch, Mademoiselle Gamay called me in to the kitchen, where we ate fish soup and slices of thick, chunky bread.

✦ ✦ ✦

It was about six o'clock when Dr. Drake and Beatrice returned. I was glad to see them, for I had actually started to get rather lonely. But my gladness soon turned to jealousy when I saw that Beatrice, although she must have spent the entire day walking, was smiling broadly, and chattering animatedly to Dr. Drake.

"Good afternoon, Daniel!" called Dr. Drake, grinning at me. "And how have you spent the day?"

I showed him the book I had been reading.

"An excellent choice!" he enthused. "Did you find it interesting?"

"I thought it was a bit difficult, but there were some interesting drawings in it," I said.

"You liked the drawings?" said Dr. Drake, smiling. "You are getting on well, I see. I shall test you on the chapters you have read after dinner, and we will see if you can have it finished by the end of the week."

My heart sank. If I had to finish that great long book, there was no way I was going out.

When he had left the room, Beatrice turned to me and said, "Cheer up, Daniel! You know, Dr. Drake isn't quite as bad as—"

"Hang Dr. Drake!" I shouted. "And hang you, too!" And I stomped out into the garden to look at the rabbits.

My mood didn't improve during the whole three days that it took me to struggle through *On the Origin of Species*. But on the fourth day, an oxcart arrived with Emery, another man, and a boy in it. On the back of the cart was what seemed to be a large crate covered in a black tarpaulin.

"Hey, Daniel!" said Emery when he saw me. "Is Dr. Drake at home?"

"He went to Horsham with my sister," I said.

"What about Dominique?" asked Emery, climbing down from the cart.

"Do you mean Mademoiselle Gamay?" I said. "She has gone out, too. They have left me behind, as usual."

He nodded and then whistled. "Well, that sure is a shame! By the way," he said, gesturing towards his companions, "This is Mr. Flyte, and this is Darcy Kemp."

Mr. Flyte, who was much older than Emery and had a bald head, nodded, while Darcy Kemp, who wore large spectacles and was dressed in clothes that were ever so slightly tatty, with a cap and a necktie done up in a knot round his throat, came over and shook me warmly by the hand.

"Delighted!" he said. "You here for the school?"

I nodded.

"We're early," said Darcy.

"Better early than late," said Mr. Flyte. "But better late than never! We shall just have to leave our cargo in the coal shed."

"You'll tell him his delivery has arrived, won't you, Daniel?" said Emery. "If he comes back before Darcy. Darcy has an errand to run."

I nodded. And then I watched the three of them as they lifted the heavy crate off the oxcart with some difficulty. Being careful not to let the tarpaulin slip, they took it over to one of the large outbuildings that seemed to have been used as a coal shed. Emery took out a key and unlocked it, and they pulled the crate inside.

When he came out, Emery said, "Now, Daniel, there's no need for a young fellow to go snooping around in there. But I know what young fellows are like!" And with a broad smile, he locked the door again and pocketed the key.

And with that, the two men got back onto the oxcart, turned it around, and set off down the long drive towards the main road. Darcy winked at me and set off in exactly the opposite direction, towards the forest.

"See you later," he said.

When I was sure they had all gone, I went back into the house and shut the door. I took up my book and started to read it, but I couldn't concentrate. I just had to find out what was in that crate. I knew there was a little window around the back of the shed with a broken latch, because I had managed to climb through it a couple of days before. Inside, it had been empty apart from a few old sacks, some coal, and three wooden beams stacked against a wall. So I went out to the shed and, trying my best not to get my clothes dirty, climbed in and went over to look at the crate. I lifted the tarpaulin that covered it, and a deafening screech sounded, making me stumble backwards towards the window.

For inside the crate was a creature that could only be described as a baby dragon—the same one that had tried to attack me in London. It was clawing at the bars of the cage, shaking it and rocking it backwards and forwards most worryingly, beating its wings and looking at me so piercingly that I could not take my gaze from it even for a moment. I felt just as a frog must feel when it is being hypnotised by a snake. I couldn't move a muscle. All I could do was gaze into the creature's eyes as a wisp of smoke curled up from its nostrils.

CHAPTER SEVEN
SCORCHER

Leaving children and hungry dragons alone together
is not an arrangement that has very much to
recommend it.

—— Dr. Drake's Dragon Diary, May 1843

The first thing that anyone who has ever studied dragons is likely to find out is that they can be extremely unpredictable. It is hard to know whether they will take a liking to you or not without actually putting yourself at risk. This was only the second time that I had seen a dragon, but from its size, even I could tell that it was only a baby. I guessed that it had been clawing at the cage because it wanted to get out. But there was something sadder and droopier about it than I would have expected in a terrifying fire-breathing monster. As I looked more closely, I noticed that it had sticky yellow phlegm dripping from its nose. Yet it was a fascinating creature. Its jet-black eyes were alive with intelligence. I just couldn't resist staring into them.

Some time later, I vaguely heard Dr. Drake and Beatrice returning from their trip. I heard them go into the house. Then I heard them come out again and call my name over and over. They sounded anxious. I should have called back, but I couldn't. All I wanted to do was look into those black eyes. Something inside made me desperate to free the dragon. I began fumbling with the lock.

Then Dr. Drake burst into the shed and quickly pulled the tarpaulin back over the crate. The moment the dragon was out of sight, I came to myself again. I started to feel frightened and backed over to the door.

"I'm sorry, little Scorcher," said Dr. Drake, lifting the tarpaulin just enough so that he could peer underneath it. "I'm afraid you are going to have to stay here until I can get something a bit more fireproof fixed up for you. But I have brought you a treat at least!"

He took out a bag and pushed one or two pieces of meat through the bars, which the baby dragon devoured hungrily.

He carefully watched it eat, as though he was evaluating its condition. Then he did something really strange. He began to sing the dragon a soft, gently lilting song that seemed to send it to sleep. I could not make out any of the words but it felt strangely comforting.

Dr. Drake replaced the tarpaulin and said to me quietly, "You are an extremely disobedient boy, Daniel. You do not have any idea of the disastrous consequences that your actions could have. You have no idea how dangerous creatures like this can be. I had thought that studying some interesting books would have helped to curb at least some of your insatiable curiosity, but I now see that I was wrong. Come and see me in my study at eight o'clock. Now, have you any questions?"

"Can I ask you about the dragon, sir?" I said.

"All that I can tell you about the dragon, Daniel, is that he was left on my doorstep in London, that I have seen him before, that his name is Scorcher, and that he is sick, which is highly unusual in a dragon. I have some skill in healing dragons, however, which is why I have been out in the forest collecting special herbs."

"How do you know so much about dragons?" I said.

"That is simple, Daniel," said Dr. Drake. "I am a *dragonologist*."

And with that, he led me out of the coal shed and back to the house, where Beatrice was very glad to see me. I was still upset that she had spent so much more time with Dr. Drake than I had, so I ignored her by pretending to read about the history of benzene in the manufacturing industries until she said, "Daniel, that book is upside down."

"Is it?" I said, without bothering to turn it over. "Of course, you won't believe me as usual, but Dr. Drake is looking after a baby dragon."

"I know," she said.

Suddenly I felt myself getting really angry.

"You *know*?" I said. "So you believe in dragons now?"

"Yes," said Beatrice. "I would never have believed in them, of course, but then I actually saw one in the wild."

I was thunderstruck.

"You saw one in the wild?"

"Yes, Daniel. The one in the forest seems a bit dumb. I was scared at first, but Dr. Drake says it's all right as long as you are careful."

"But why is he teaching you about dragons and not me?" I shouted.

"But he will teach you! That's what the summer school is all about. He is just very upset that you went sneaking round his shop without—"

"Oh, come off it!" I said. "I was looking for him. Could anyone *not* have looked through that keyhole when they heard all that screeching and roaring? Could anyone *not* have looked in the coal shed, knowing what was inside?"

"But dragons are dangerous, Daniel. All you have to do is prove to Dr. Drake that he can trust you, and he will teach you all about them. And I've found out that he isn't a 'dracocologist' at all. He's a dragonologist."

"I *know*," I said.

At dinner that night Darcy joined us for the first time. He looked happy as he came out of Dr. Drake's study. Obviously whatever errand he had been on had been a success.

"So you are going to study dragons, too?" he said to us as we waited for the adults to arrive.

"Yes," said Beatrice. "Will it just be us three?"

"No," said Darcy. "Last year there was another boy. This year he's bringing his sister."

"What are they like?" asked Beatrice.

"Well, they're rich," said Darcy. "But they're all right. The girl is named Alicia, and the boy is named William. Everyone calls him Billy, though. He's got some funny ideas, but don't let that worry you. They're the son and daughter of Lord Chiddingfold. He's a man in the government. He's the Minister for—"

"Thank you, Darcy," said Dr. Drake, who had just come in. "I am glad to see you three have been introducing yourselves. But class does not begin for a few days yet."

After dinner, at eight o'clock, I knocked on the door of Dr. Drake's study.

"Come in, Daniel," he said.

And so in I went. Dr. Drake was sitting behind a large desk, with a pen in his hand.

"I shall only be a moment," he said. "Do sit down."

I sat on a chair facing the desk. Dr. Drake went back to his work. He was writing what seemed to be a very long and formal-looking letter, and I had a chance to look around his study. It had hundreds of books ranged on tall shelves that ran right round the room. On the wall there was a large painting of Saint George and the Dragon and several other small paintings and sketches. At the end of the study, behind the desk, was a padlocked door. But what held my attention were some sheets of paper that lay on Dr. Drake's desk. One was a letter in a thin, slanting hand. The other was a sort of painted diagram of a gemstone. In the very centre of the gemstone was what looked like the reflection of an old man with an extremely long beard. Even though it was upside down, I could read the caption above it, which said, *The Dragon's Eye*. What also interested me was that I could see the signature on the letter next to it: *Ignatius Crook*.

I am not very good at reading things upside down, but I did my best. I managed to make out a few phrases like *My Dear Ernest; my father, Ebenezer;* and *our most valuable family treasures,* before Dr. Drake put down his pen and shuffled the papers on his desk so that the sketch of the Dragon's Eye disappeared from view. Then, he stood up, gesturing over to an umbrella stand in the corner, which contained a large assortment of canes, sticks, and three-foot-long metal rulers. I feared for the worst.

"Choose one," he said simply.

I went over to the umbrella stand with a heavy heart and carefully chose the lightest-looking cane I could find. I presented it to Dr. Drake with a downcast expression.

"But that one's no good, Daniel," cried Dr. Drake. "What? Did you think I was going to beat you? I don't go in for punishments of *that* sort, my boy. Instead, I have decided I cannot quite trust you at the moment and so I am going to keep you with me. You will be able to indulge your curiosity to the full. You are going to both see and learn a lot of things you have never even dreamt of. So you must choose a stick that will be useful for beating back thick undergrowth. You must take the notebook and pencil that I am going to give you and write *Daniel Cook's Dragonological Record Book* on the first page. And you must be up and ready to leave the house at five o'clock tomorrow morning."

After helping me to choose a much stouter stick, which looked perfect for beating back even the thickest briars, Dr. Drake showed me to my room and bade me good night. Darcy was already sleeping in one of the other beds. I was very tired too. Yet I was so anxious to have my first lesson in dragonology that I have never had so little sleep in all my life as I had that night. I crept quietly out of the room and was ready and waiting for Dr. Drake in the hallway with my record book and my stick in my hand at half past four.

Chapter Eight
WEASEL

My first dragon didn't breathe fire, couldn't fly, and
didn't even have proper wings. But I was
completely enthralled.
—— Dr. Drake's Dragon Diary, August 1844

When he arrived at five o'clock, Dr. Drake was carrying the same leather bag I had often seen him carry, a stout stick of his own, and a glass bottle full of some kind of honey-coloured liquid with a label that read, Dr. Drake's Linctus. He unlatched the front door, and we slipped out.

"Daniel," he whispered, "the first lesson a dragonologist must learn is that once there were a great many dragons, but now there are far fewer. Although fully grown dragons are indeed powerful and dangerous, they are, as a species, no match for human beings. There is a danger that they may even become extinct. So the first lesson a dragonologist must learn is to conserve and protect those dragons that still remain, wherever he can."

"Is that what the linctus is for?" I asked him.

"As I told you, Scorcher is sick. It is strange because dragons hardly ever get ill, and I have not encountered this particular sickness in dragons before. But the linctus seems to be helping. Scorcher has brightened up considerably. Soon I will be able to take him home."

"Do you know where he comes from, then?"

"Yes."

"Did someone steal him?"

"I am afraid so, Daniel. I did not realise until this morning exactly who it was or quite what it was they wanted. But now I see a great danger coming, not only for dragonologists, but for ordinary people and dragons, too."

"Was it Ignatius Crook?" I asked.

"Wait for me here," said Dr. Drake. "I must go and give Scorcher his medicine."

When he came back, the bottle of linctus was empty. Dr. Drake put it down next to the front door. Then he peered at me closely, in much the same way he had peered at Scorcher the day before, and gestured for me to follow him. We headed up the drive and along the path that led into the forest. There we walked silently for some distance—it may have been about two miles—before Dr. Drake paused and offered me a cheese sandwich and a drink of lemonade from a bottle that he was carrying in his bag.

"Now," said Dr. Drake when we had both eaten, "have you heard of the Knucker Hole?"

I had to admit that I hadn't.

"It is a very deep pool about thirty miles from here that lies just outside of the village of Lyminster, near the south coast. People used to say that the pool was so deep that it actually had no bottom. They also used to say that it was the home of a dragon. But only one of those two things was correct."

"The part about the dragon?" I asked.

"Indeed. The dragon that lived there used to be what is called a knucker. They are quite small for dragons. They are long and thin, and they have very small wings and cannot actually fly. But I don't want to tell you too much at the moment, as I need you to find out everything you can on your own. Take out your record book, and make a note of your first assignment: tonight I want you to make a list of all the differences you notice between the knucker and Scorcher, who is a European dragon. Providing you can remember much about Scorcher, of course." He said.

"I remember Scorcher's eyes quite well," I said.

"Really?" said Dr. Drake. "I would have thought that his fangs, wings, tail, scales, or the smoke coming from his nostrils—which is quite a remarkable phenomenon for such a young dragon, by the way—would have been more memorable. In order to compare the two dragons, you are going to have to meet a knucker. And while there is no knucker at Lyminster anymore, there is one here in the forest, which I have been studying for quite some time. When I am at home, I like to make a daily record of her behaviour, and I am going to introduce you. I call her Weasel."

"Does Weasel live in a pool, too?" I asked.

"No. A knucker does not always need a pool. Weasel has a hole in the side of one of the streambeds. Knuckers are very lazy. Weasel is happy living here because the soil is mostly sand, which is easy to dig burrows in, and she is rather partial to rabbit. But I would be careful not to get too close to her until she gets to know you. It is sometimes said that a hungry knucker will take a stray child for its dinner, if it finds one. Now, I am going to tell you no more about knuckers, but I want you to note down everything you see.

"Dragonology, as I am sure you realise, is not a very well known area of study, and most books about it are not at all reliable. So a dragonologist's record book—or dragon diary—becomes his most precious resource, with information on everything he has ever learned or found out about dragons, and notes on all the different things he plans to find out as soon as he can. When you study a live dragon, it is particularly important to record the time, the weather conditions, the sort of dragon you are studying, and any dragon behaviours that you note, including whether it can talk or not."

I must have looked surprised—and probably rather sceptical at this—because Dr. Drake continued: "Dragons are practically the only creatures, apart from humans and unicorns, of course, that can talk. Not all of them have this ability, however. Knuckers generally don't, but there have been some exceptions. But to find out anything, of course, you have to find the knucker. Which means a spot of tracking. Why don't you look around? I suggest starting with some soft ground."

Dr. Drake gestured with his stick, and I climbed down a steep bank and through some thick undergrowth to where I could hear the trickling stream. I was amazed to discover a set of large lizardlike footprints in the sandy mud.

"You must make a record of what those tracks look like, Daniel," said Dr. Drake. "Draw a picture of them. Then you will be able to recognise them again. Try to show how deep the various bits press into the sand, and make sure you get the proportions right."

And so I bent down to study the tracks and drew a careful picture of the clearest of the tracks as best I could. There were three long, thin toe marks at the front, each with a claw at the end that had made only the lightest of impressions. There was a deep pad mark and another mark left by the beast's single hind claw. When I had finished, I showed my work to Dr. Drake.

"Excellent," he said. "Now follow the tracks."

So I stepped over the narrow stream and followed the tracks up to where they disappeared among the leafy bracken.

"Be careful, Daniel!" whispered Dr. Drake behind me.

I peered ahead into the gloom and realised that there was something slithering gently ahead of me through the undergrowth. It was the knucker.

"Weasel is hunting rabbits," whispered Dr. Drake. "She almost always hunts in the early morning."

As I edged forwards, I trod on a stick, which broke with a loud snap and caused Weasel to stop and raise her head. As she turned towards me, I could see that she had two bright, snakelike eyes. But her eyes didn't have the intelligence of Scorcher's eyes.

"Be careful, Daniel," said Dr. Drake in a loud whisper. "Stay absolutely still."

I stayed as still as I could. The knucker, which must have been very used to Dr. Drake by now, glanced over at him and then ignored us. I studied her carefully. She was leathery brown and seemed to have skin rather than scales. I could see two little bunches near her front legs, which must have been the useless wings Dr. Drake had mentioned.

Meanwhile Weasel continued her rabbit hunt. She slithered into a thick patch of undergrowth, her attention fixed on a patch of grass. Several rabbits, which had been disturbed by the noises I had made, had returned to feed. Weasel's head quivered in anticipation as she watched one particularly fat-looking rabbit hop over to join two others on a patch of clover. Suddenly she leapt forwards, her tail flicked around behind, and her snakelike body curled into three loops, which she dropped neatly over the three rabbits' heads. Soon they were dangling from the loops in Weasel's body like clothes bobbing on a washing line. Then, with three quick gulps, they were gone. The knucker stretched, gave a happy little shudder and wiggle, then slithered away.

"Now," said Dr. Drake, when Weasel had gone, "that is your first lesson completed. I would like you to complete the first entries in your record book by this evening if possible."

And with that, we returned through the forest, and back to Castle Drake.

When we arrived, I found Beatrice sitting at a little table in the drawing room. She was reading a book, and I saw that she had a record book just like mine, lying open beside her, with a dictionary next to it. She seemed to have completed quite a large entry on the knucker already. She looked up.

"How was your trip?" she asked. "Did you track Weasel, then watch her hunting?"

"Yes," I said.

"Well, tomorrow Dr. Drake will probably take you to Weasel's lair," she said, smiling. "I was wondering if you could help me. I'm having a bit of trouble with the idea behind this book. Dr. Drake says that you understand it quite well, but I'm not sure where to begin."

She showed the book to me. It was Darwin's *On the Origin of Species.*

"Are you studying that too, then?" I asked.

"Yes," said Beatrice. "Dr. Drake says that it's exactly the sort of thing a dragonologist needs to understand in order to study dragons in what he calls 'the proper scientific manner.'"

I felt pleased that Beatrice needed my help, so I said, "Well, as far as I can see, Darwin visited some islands called the Galápagos, where he noticed that different tortoises and birds were slightly different on different islands. So he came up with a theory. All baby animals are born with small differences between them. One may be bigger, another faster, or another may just have a longer neck. If those differences give them an advantage over other animals—in defending themselves, perhaps, or in finding food—then they are more likely to survive until they have babies themselves, and the babies may well exhibit the same traits. Over millions of years, these differences can grow and grow until the animals become so different that they can turn into a completely new species. It's called natural selection."

"Thank you, Daniel," said Beatrice.

Beatrice went back to reading the book and occasionally looking up words in the dictionary, which was something that, annoyingly, I hadn't thought of when I'd been trying to read it. I took out my record book and, pencil in hand, opened a new page and laid out my records as I had been taught by Dr. Drake:

DRAGON: *Knucker*
NAME: *Weasel*
DETAILS: *Leathery brown, looks like a large snake—but with legs. Small head, big ears. Two small wings in bunches near front legs—apparently useless (something to do with evolution?). Sort of arrow at end of tail. Body seems slimy—damp from stream?*
DATE: *August 2, 1882*
LOCATION: *St. Leonard's Forest*
WEATHER CONDITIONS: *Bright and sunny*

TIME: *About half past six in the morning*

OBSERVATIONS: *Weasel seems to like hunting in the early morning. She moves very quietly, although she seems to move in a sort of half slide, half walk. She creeps up on a group of rabbits, and then sort of makes a dash into the middle of them. Amazingly, she can catch three at a time, wrapping her body around each one to kill it by constriction. Then she swallows them whole and slithers off back towards the stream, where her hole must be.*

When I had completed the record of everything I had seen, I made a new entry listing the differences between Weasel and Scorcher.

ADULT KNUCKER	BABY EUROPEAN DRAGON
"Weasel"	*"Scorcher"*
15 feet long	*2½ feet long*
Doesn't breathe fire	*Breathes smoke (fire later?)*
Small wings; cannot fly	*Large wings (learning to fly?)*

Leathery skin	Reddish scales
Long and thin	More dragon-shaped
Arrow-headed tail	Arrow-headed tail
Four legs	Four legs

CHAPTER NINE
FIELD DRAGONOLOGY

The wonderful world of dragonology is open to
everyone —— even so-called scientists —— if they
would only go out and look!
—— Dr. Drake's Dragon Diary, August 1844

For the next few days, I got up early with Dr. Drake to go and study Weasel. On the second day, after watching her feed again, Dr. Drake let me track her to her lair and taught me how to tell the difference between fresh tracks, which are unbroken, and tracks that have crumbly edges or tiny bits of twig or grass over them, which are a day old or more. He made me crouch among the bracken, looking for signs of hidden tracks such as broken stems, or bits of slime where Weasel's tail had rubbed against the boles of trees. He also taught me how to track the knucker from upwind, so that she would not smell me coming.

When I reached Weasel's lair, I saw that it was dug among some tree roots by the edge of the stream, in one of the deepest parts of the forest. Small piles of what looked like fur and bones lay scattered round. I rushed to examine one, but Dr. Drake called me back.

"Daniel," he said, "a dragonologist must remember to remain concealed when approaching a dragon, particularly one in its own lair. It can be highly dangerous to introduce yourself too soon. Even though this knucker knows me and is unlikely to attack us, you ought always to follow this practise so that you will be prepared if you have to attract the attention of an unknown dragon."

I nodded, and Dr. Drake then reached into his bag and handed me two small parcels covered with waxed paper. One of them contained sliced onions, while the other was full of sausages.

"Now," said Dr. Drake, "a dragon can often be tempted to the mouth of its lair by offering it a suitable gift. With a more intelligent specimen, such as Scorcher, this might involve something shiny, since European dragons love to collect treasure. However, he is only a juvenile, so it is unlikely that he is yet able to tell the difference between true gemstones and shiny bits of glass. Weasel is a much simpler creature, so food will have to suffice. I mixed up the onions and sausages overnight, so the onions should have taken on some of their smell. Throw them towards the mouth of the lair."

I did this and was not surprised to see Weasel's head emerge from the hole, twisting about until she spied the parcel of onions, which she sniffed. She did not seem very pleased. In fact she came halfway out of her lair, padding to the left and right, arching her back and making a whining noise like an angry pig.

"Now," said Dr. Drake, "throw the parcel of sausages."

When the sausages landed, Weasel bent down and sniffed them, arched her back again, gave a sort of little whinny of pleasure, and gobbled them down in one go. Then she wriggled back into her lair.

"Now that Weasel knows we mean her no harm, we may move just a little closer," said Dr. Drake.

We went over to examine one of the piles of bones and fur. It looked very much as though it had come from one of the rabbits.

"What do you make of that?" he asked.

"Well," I suggested, "Weasel eats her food whole, so maybe she regurgitates what she can't digest, like an owl?"

"Indeed," said Dr. Drake. "But you must be careful. Look."

And he pointed with his stick to several small round drops of purple goo that had dripped onto the bones.

"That is knucker venom. As well as being able to kill its prey by constriction, the knucker also has a highly venomous bite. If you were to accidentally touch that venom with unbroken skin, it would not do much damage, but if it were to get into a cut or into your mouth or eyes, then you would have a problem. A small amount would most likely not kill you, but it would be a rather nasty experience and you would be incapacitated for several weeks."

✦ ✦ ✦

On the third day, Dr. Drake took me to the lair while Weasel was out hunting. He had brought a long coil of rope with a weight and a net on the end. He asked me to cast it into the mouth of the lair and see what I could bring out.

"Remember that we do not have much time," he said. "We do not want to be caught stealing from a dragon's lair."

I threw the weight down into the hole. It took the rope and the net with it. Although the rope was long, there was a jerk, as if the weight had fallen down a vertical shaft.

"Don't let go," said Dr. Drake as nearly the whole of the rope disappeared down the hole. I gradually pulled it back out, hand over hand. The net must have caught something, for it felt heavy. At last I pulled the net out of the hole and dumped out its contents. I don't know what I had expected to find—treasure, perhaps, or maybe more rabbit bones, but all I found were several old glass bottles and about ten clay pipes.

"All right," said Dr. Drake. "Now you must put it back."

And so I used my stick to push the bottles and pipes back down the hole. Then Dr. Drake opened his leather bag and took out three more old-looking clay pipes and one of his empty linctus bottles and laid them near the mouth of the lair.

"The knucker will know we have been here, so perhaps leaving her some gifts will make up for it," he said.

When we were on the way back home, Dr. Drake asked, "What do you make of that, Daniel?"

I didn't know what to answer.

"That knuckers like to smoke and drink?" I said, smiling.

"Dear me, Daniel," said Dr. Drake, laughing. "Knuckers may be stupid in dragon terms, but they are not that stupid. The important thing to learn is that all dragons love to hoard treasure. Now, knuckers aren't very particular about what they hoard. They will take almost any small objects that humans leave lying round, as long as they can drag them into their lair. And all Weasel has managed to find is an old rubbish heap."

On the fourth day, Dr. Drake announced that Darcy and Beatrice were going to come along. By now I was spending the afternoons discussing with Beatrice what she had seen and comparing it to my own experiences. Beatrice was making great strides with Darwin and had copied several of the dragon pictures into her record book.

"I wish there were a book on dragonology," she said as we were waiting by the front door for Dr. Drake to appear. "I'd like to see pictures of some of the different species of dragon Dr. Drake talks about."

Darcy arrived. He had overheard Beatrice, and he smiled.

"Well, tomorrow you may be in luck," he said. "Dragon school is starting. This will be our last day before classes begin and today, Dr. Drake wants me to take you out into the forest. Our goal is to find out just how far Weasel ranges, so we have to look out for all the signs that we can. And we have to be careful," he added.

"Isn't Dr. Drake coming with us?" asked Beatrice.

"No," said Darcy. "But don't worry. I'm sure we'll be safe. Weasel will recognise your smell by now, and we have a map of the forest."

He led the way, but instead of heading towards Weasel's lair, we headed towards the part of the stream where I had first seen her.

"Now," said Darcy, "since no one has managed to record any knucker tracks farther down the stream than here, we can be pretty sure this is as far as she goes. Dr. Drake wants us to estimate her range and mark it on the map. Has anyone got any ideas?"

Beatrice thought for a moment and said, "How about plotting Weasel's lair on the map, and then setting off in a circle around it, looking for tracks and signs?"

Darcy and I both agreed, and we headed towards the lair. After marking it on the map, we set off through the forest in a series of spirals that got larger and larger, searching the forest in a fairly wide band. It was difficult, but occasionally we would come across faint bits of purple gloop, or darker bits that had dried on trees, or parts of the forest where there seemed to be fewer rabbits. Each time we did so, Beatrice, who had commandeered the map from Darcy, made a small X. It took us a couple of hours, but as our circles ranged farther out into the forest, we soon came to areas where there were no more signs of dragon activity. To do the job more quickly, we had spread out, and every five minutes we shouted to each other to keep in contact.

"Daniel! Don't go too far off," Darcy shouted to me when I had gone about two hundred yards on my quest to find bits of purple gloop in the woods.

"I won't!" I shouted back. But then I saw something just a bit farther on that intrigued me, so I went to investigate. It was a tall fence that had been broken down. It seemed to be an enclosure of some kind. Just beyond it were several trees that had long gashes scored in them. I could tell that the gashes were quite recent, because sap was still dripping from the cuts. I assumed that they were evidence of the knucker sharpening its claws, but I wasn't sure, since I hadn't seen any other trees like that. I took out my record book and had begun to sketch the gashes when Darcy and Beatrice came running up.

"Didn't you hear us calling?" said Beatrice.

"Look what I've found," I said, pointing to the broken fence and the claw marks.

Darcy looked rather shocked when he saw the fence.

"We've gone too far," he said.

"But weren't these gashes made by Weasel?" I asked.

"No, that's not a knucker. Knuckers don't sharpen their claws like that. They use bits of stone or flint, or the bricks around the edge of wells."

Suddenly, there was a thunderous roar. We all jumped. It was much too loud to have come from Weasel.

"It must be another dragon!" I said.

"Let's go," said Darcy.

"Shouldn't we find out what it is?" I asked.

"No," said Darcy. "We must get home as quickly as possible."

And he would say no more but led us back towards Castle Drake as fast as he could. I looked back. A plume of grey smoke was rising up through the trees.

When we arrived, we were greeted with the sight of a carriage coming up the driveway.

"That will be Billy and Alicia," said Darcy. "Say hello to them for me, won't you?" And he rushed into the house.

Chapter Ten
THE SOCIETY OF DRAGONOLOGISTS

Dealing in dragons, or dragon eggs, ought to be
vigorously discouraged and the felonious
perpetrators encouraged to see the error of their ways.
—— Dr. Drake's Dragon Diary, November 1845

The carriage that pulled up to the front door of Castle Drake looked very smart and the boy and girl who got down from it were well dressed, the boy in an Eton jacket and the girl in a long dress that did not look at all suitable for tramping about in an overgrown forest.

"Daniel Cook, I presume?" said the boy. "Delighted. And your sister, of course." At which he shook us both by the hand and continued, "Billy's the name. This is my sister."

The girl shook us both by the hand as well and said shyly, "I'm Alicia."

"And I'm Beatrice," said Beatrice.

"And jolly good dragonologists you'll make, I expect," said Billy. "Is Dr. Drake about?"

But when we went into the house, there was no sign of Dr. Drake or Darcy or even Mademoiselle Gamay.

"Well, I am sure they are going to be back soon," said Billy. "Are you members of the S.A.S.D. yet?"

I didn't know what the S.A.S.D. was, so I shook my head.

"I don't think so," said Beatrice.

"Never mind," he said. "I expect you will be joining soon enough."

"Joining what?" asked Beatrice.

"The S.A.S.D., of course," said Billy.

"It means the Secret and Ancient Society of Dragonologists," said Alicia.

"I've never heard of it," said Beatrice.

"That's because it's secret," said Billy, "obviously."

"Does it have many members?" I asked.

"Oh, no," said Billy. "There's my father and Dr. Drake and Emery and Mademoiselle Gamay. And your parents, of course."

"Our parents?" said Beatrice.

"Of course," said Billy. "Isn't that why you're here? Dr. Drake doesn't teach just anyone about dragons. It's restricted."

"Who restricts it?" I asked.

"My father mainly," he said. "He's the Minister for Dragons."

"The Minister for Dragons?"

"Yes," said Billy. "My father is Lewis Light, Lord

Chiddingfold. They call him a Minister without Portfolio, but everyone in the S.A.S.D. knows he's the Minister for Dragons.

"So the government knows about dragons?" said Beatrice incredulously.

"Only a few people. There's the Prime Minister, of course."

"William Gladstone?"

"Yes. And then there's the Queen. They say that she finds the idea of dragons quite amusing. But most people don't know anything about dragons at all, and that's the way my father says it has to stay. It's for the dragons' own good as much as for the people, you see."

"I think we must have seen someone from the government when were at Dr. Drake's shop in London," said Beatrice. "He had a very red face."

"Oh, that would have been Mr. Tibbs," said Billy. "He is Father's Secretary. There's been quite a rumpus about a dragon that Dr. Drake is supposed to have brought to London. My father nearly had second thoughts about letting me come here this year, but then I'm his man on the inside, you see." He winked. "I'm quite anxious to see Scorcher, though."

"Yes," I said. "But Dr. Drake didn't bring him to London. He was dumped on his doorstep."

"I'm sure he was," said Billy, "But it's a bit strange, isn't it? Just dumping a dragon on someone's doorstep?"

"And what about our parents?" said Beatrice.

"Well, normally they would have told you about the

S.A.S.D. on your fourteenth birthday," said Billy. "Haven't they said anything at all?"

"They are in India," said Beatrice. "Our father works there."

There was a pause. A look of surprise passed over Billy's face.

"You really don't know, do you?" he said.

We both looked blank.

"Then I'm sorry if it comes as a shock, but your parents are in India acting as dragonological investigators. At this moment they are investigating a strange illness that seems to have taken hold among the nagas of the Thar Desert in India. It seems to have taken a turn for the worse, which is why they haven't been able to return this summer as they had expected. But look on the bright side. It does mean that you get to come to Dr. Drake's summer school and learn about dragons."

"I knew Dr. Drake had something to do with their going away," said Beatrice.

"Well, don't blame me," said Billy. "In any case, where is he? I expect he's off in the forest somewhere. Shall we go and see if we can find him?"

"I think I shall just stay here," said Beatrice.

Alicia, who hadn't said anything during our whole conversation, said that she would stay as well. This cheered Beatrice up.

"Have you learned about dragons, too?" she said.

"This is my first year," said Alicia. "Last year, it was just Billy and Darcy. So I only know what Billy has told me. But he doesn't have a terribly high opinion of girls, so he said I probably wouldn't remember anything. He says he can't really understand the point in us studying dragons at all as we're only going to go and get married and have babies."

Billy smiled and shrugged. I looked over at Beatrice. I could see that she was not happy.

"Father wants me to be here," said Alicia.

"Only because Dr. Drake made him promise," said Billy.

There was a pause. Beatrice put her hands on her hips and turned to Alicia with a smile.

"I think you and I ought to have a talk," she said.

Soon Billy and I were heading off into the forest.

"I saw some strange dragon tracks," I said. "I think we might find Dr. Drake there."

"I wouldn't be surprised," said Billy. "I saw you and Darcy rushing through the woods as we pulled onto the drive. Darcy looked worried. Assuming that the stupid knucker is behaving herself, then unless I'm mistaken, Jamal has got out again."

"Jamal?"

"You don't know anything, do you?" said Billy. "Jamal is a young wyvern. Dr. Drake is looking after him. He hatched him from the egg himself. You see, my father heard about a shady dealer from Shadwell Dock who was actually selling stolen dragon eggs in London. When he found out about it, most of the eggs had been sold to people who did all the wrong things, so they never hatched. But the shady dealer had one left, which Dr. Drake hatched, after solemnly promising my father to take it back to Africa as soon as it was old enough. Wyverns hunt elephants and things, you see. It wouldn't do to have a fully grown one in Sussex, no matter how friendly it was."

"What happened to the shady dealer?"

"Oh, they threw him in jail. But it was a bit difficult to get a conviction, having to keep his crime secret and everything, so we managed to convince him to emigrate to Australia, where he's living, near Sydney, under the watchful eye of a friendly Australian dragonologist named Dragon Man Dan. Dan gets him to do errands from time to time, checking up on the marsupial dragons and things, but they have never really taken to him. He's been knocked out at least twice. Marsupials like to box, you see. Oh well, serves him right."

By now my head was in a spin with all this new information, but I didn't have time to ask any more questions, because Dr. Drake, Darcy, and Mademoiselle Gamay were coming through the forest towards us.

Dr. Drake smiled. "Good morning, Billy," he said.

"How is Jamal?" asked Billy.

"Oh, he is fine," said Dr. Drake. "Just fine."

And he gave me a big wink.

Chapter Eleven
THE FIVE *F*'S

Fieldwork, foresight, forwardness, frankness, and the
avoidance of fatalities are the rock-hard foundations
upon which all dragonological study must be built.
—— Dr. Drake's Dragon Diary, February 1846

At nine o'clock the next morning I found myself in a state
of great excitement, sitting at a desk in one of the outbuildings near Castle Drake. Inside were three rows of
wooden desks with inkwells. Billy chose a seat at the front of
the class with Darcy, while Beatrice, Alicia, and I took seats
in the second row. We each had our dragonological record
books with us. I noticed that Billy's and Darcy's both looked
particularly thick and that Darcy's had even spilled over into
a second volume. The classroom was a bit stuffy, as though it
had not been opened for a while, and there was a small table
to one side with a collection of scientific equipment on it.
There was a microscope, some test tubes, a few dried herbs,
and some glass jars, one of which seemed to contain a black-

and-yellow lizard that appeared to have six feet preserved in some kind of greenish liquid. Around the walls were various pictures. One showed a dragon's skeletal structure, while another seemed to be a sort of spotter's guide, showing silhouettes of different kinds of dragon. But what interested me most was a large map of the world that had small pictures of dragons tacked onto it in various places.

Dr. Drake came in and stood near the blackboard at the front of the classroom. He was followed by Mademoiselle Gamay and by Emery, who had returned to Castle Drake that morning.

"Good morning, children," said Dr. Drake with a smile.

"Good morning, Dr. Drake," we chorused.

"Now, then," he continued, "I would like to begin our summer school in dragonology by making a few comments on the role of a dragonologist. As you all know, dragons are particularly rare animals, unloved by science and championed, in the main, by the deluded and the decidedly eccentric. However, while it would not be wise for the whole world to know that we are living in close proximity to a large number of ferocious, terrifying, fire-breathing creatures, there are a few—who go by the name of dragonologists— whose task is to find them, to befriend them where possible, and to study them.

"Given that dragons are so scarce, this study—or rather science—has one chief aim, which is to promote the conservation and protection of dragons wherever possible. That is why you, Billy, and you, Darcy, have both sworn the binding Oath of a Dragonologist. Alicia, Beatrice, and Daniel, you must now swear the same oath in order to be admitted as junior and as yet unfledged members of the Secret and Ancient Society of Dragonologists. I would ask you to step forward."

Alicia rose from her seat, and Beatrice and I followed her. It all seemed very strange. I had never been asked to swear any oaths at school before now, except for the usual sort about doing my duty to my country and that kind of thing.

"Alicia," said Dr. Drake, "I see that Billy has completed his homework for the year by giving you some basic instruction about dragons. Beatrice and Daniel, you have learned a little bit about dragons as well. I think that Weasel has made a very good start for you. I must now ask you if you are ready to learn more about them. In order to do so you must each swear the Oath of a Dragonologist in the presence of two witnesses." Here he nodded towards Mademoiselle Gamay and Emery.

"What do you think?" whispered Beatrice to me.

"Well, I don't think it can do any harm," I replied. "Our parents must have sworn this oath, too."

We nodded to Dr. Drake, who asked Alicia to repeat the oath after him: "I, Alicia Light, do solemnly swear to conserve and protect those dragons that still remain, and in no way to harm them or reveal their secret hiding places to those who do not believe in them or would wish them anything other than good fortune."

When Alicia had made the oath, Dr. Drake asked Beatrice and me to repeat it after him as well.

"Now," he said, "welcome to the Secret and Ancient Society of Dragonologists. Emery and Mademoiselle Gamay will leave us now, but they are both excellent dragonologists, and they will be teaching some of the lessons that you will learn here. As you may or may not know, there are various levels of dragonological achievement, beginning with Dragonological Apprentice and continuing through Dragonological Alumnus—which is the level Billy and Darcy have attained—to Dragonologist Second Class, Dragonologist First Class, and finally Dragon Master, which is, as we speak, a theoretical honour, for there has been no Dragon Master of the Secret and Ancient Society of Dragonologists for a number of years."

"Aren't you a Dragon Master, then?" I asked.

"I'm afraid not," said Dr. Drake, smiling. "In the first place, it is the dragons themselves who decide who is to become Dragon Master. In the second, before the last Dragon Master died, he decided, along with the then Minister for Dragons, Lord Chiddingfold's father, that the Secret and Ancient Society should not recommend anyone for that role. I'm rather afraid that dragons were becoming a little too well-known, and the last Dragon Master did not quite see eye to eye with me on the subject of what I call dragon science. You see, I feel that the best way to help conserve and protect dragons is for people to learn about them. The last

Dragon Master felt the same way until he began to teach rather a lot of people about dragons and found things going horribly wrong. He decided that it was safer if people didn't know about dragons at all. He and the government decided that the existence of dragons must be kept secret at all costs and that, if dragons died out, then that must be their destiny."

"That was Ebenezer Crook, wasn't it, sir?" asked Billy.

"Yes," said Dr. Drake.

"And my grandfather agreed with him?"

"Indeed he did. He went further, for he believed that if too many humans became aware of dragons, then a conflict would inevitably occur in which the government would find itself duty-bound to destroy all dragons as a dangerous menace to human beings. But we are getting ahead of ourselves. The *modern* history of the Society is not on our curriculum this year. You have a great deal to learn about dragons themselves. You may congratulate yourselves on being members of a very select group."

"So Ignatius Crook is the son of the last Dragon Master?" I blurted out.

"Yes," said Dr. Drake. "Ignatius is the son of Ebenezer Crook. But he is no longer a friend of the S.A.S.D. If you should ever meet him, then I should be wary of anything he says to you. In fact, I should try to avoid him if at all possible. And if you see him again, you must tell me at once."

"But why can't they just make you Dragon Master?" asked Beatrice.

"Dear me," said Dr. Drake, "if I have to answer all these questions, then we are not going to learn very much today. Suffice it to say that, even if the Minister for Dragons and I decided that the time was right, it is not just a question of calling yourself Dragon Master. As I said, the honour can only be bestowed by the dragons themselves. The most intelligent ones have their own society, you know. It is called the Society of Dragons. And there is a special artefact that is needed, which is no longer in the possession of the S.A.S.D. It is called the Dragon's Eye. Woe betide us if Ignatius Crook should ever lay his hands on it. But as I have told you far more than I needed to, do not ask me any more questions. Time is drawing on."

Mademoiselle Gamay and Emery left, and Dr. Drake, who I supposed must be a Dragonologist First Class, asked Billy to show us the "signs" of the Dragonological Apprentices. There were three of these, and they were the means by which one dragonologist could recognise another in secret. The first sign was a gesture—a fist held loosely at one's side while the index finger pointed to the ground. It could be made without drawing attention to oneself and symbolised the fact that dragonologists have sworn to conserve and protect all dragons even were there to be only one single dragon left. The second was a call for assistance—the hands were crossed and raised over the head in fists. This sign was easy to see from a distance, and dragonologists were duty-bound to answer such a call if they ever saw it.

Finally, there were the words. Billy explained that there was an ancient dragon riddle that was used as a password. Dr. Drake asked him and Darcy to demonstrate it to us.

Billy smiled. He and Darcy stood up and went to the front of the class.

"When a dragon flies . . . ?" he asked.

"He seeks it with his eyes," said Darcy.

"When a dragon roars . . . ?" asked Billy.

"He holds it in his claws," concluded Darcy.

"You see," said Dr. Drake. "It is quite simple. This is the password, but it is only the first part of the riddle. The rest of it goes like this:

When he slumbers deep, he dreams of it in sleep,
But there beneath his head, it forms his stony bed.

"Now, I wonder: Can any of you new apprentices guess the answer to that riddle?"

I thought about it. But it wasn't a very difficult riddle. I soon had the answer, and so did Beatrice and Alicia. Our hands shot up.

"What is it?" asked Dr. Drake.

"Treasure!" we chorused, smiling.

After lunch, classes in dragonology began in earnest. Dr. Drake went to the blackboard and drew a diagram showing how dragons breathed fire.

"Today," he said, "we are going to begin our lessons by remembering that dragons can be very dangerous. They can breathe fire, after all."

Dr. Drake then gave us a brief lesson on fire breathing. Apparently, some dragonologists believed the theory that dragons produce helium gas or methane, which they then ignite with a spark. In fact, as Dr. Drake pointed out, they actually spray out a fine mist of venom that has evolved so as to be flammable. They light the spray with a spark produced by knocking together a piece of rock, known as iron pyrites, and a piece of flint. They even carry these around with them in a special pouch in their mouths that has actually evolved for the purpose over millions of years.

"Some dragons must travel a great distance to find the necessary rocks to produce the spark," said Dr. Drake. "But fire breathing is just one of the ways in which dragons can be dangerous. To counter this danger, the experienced dragonologist must remember five simple words beginning with *F*. They are known as the Five *F*'s of Dragonology."

And he wrote the following words on the blackboard: *Fieldwork, Foresight, Forwardness, Frankness,* and *Fatalities.* He underlined the last word three times before turning back to us.

"Can you tell me about fieldwork, Beatrice? You have been doing some with the knucker."

"Does it mean studying dragons in the wild?" asked Beatrice.

"Well, it's a *bit* more complicated," said Billy.

"Why is that?" asked Dr. Drake.

"Well, you need a record book, and you need to remember the other four *F*'s," said Billy. "And it's best by far to study dragons in their natural environments."

"Well, yes, but I think Beatrice was on the right track, don't you?" said Dr. Drake. "And what about foresight, Darcy?"

"Proper training and preparation are absolutely essential," said Darcy.

"Forwardness, Alicia?"

"That's something to do with being brave, isn't it?" asked Alicia.

"Oh, come on!" said Billy. "I told you: 'The student must be both daring and truly courageous.'"

"Frankness, Daniel?" said Dr. Drake, raising his eyebrow a little.

"Er, a dragonologist must be frank?" I said.

"Indeed," said Dr. Drake. "Which means?"

"He must tell the truth?"

"Quite," said Dr. Drake. "A dragonologist must report honestly what he sees at all times. And as for fatalities, unless these are avoided, I'm afraid you won't make much progress at all. There is one particular danger, however, that is often forgotten. We studied it last year. Can either of you, Billy or Darcy, tell these other children what it is?"

They both looked blank.

"While a dragonologist must never underestimate the dangers of suffering from bites, burns, slashes from claws, death by constriction . . ."

"Oh," said Darcy. "Hypnosis."

"Can you remember what kinds of dragon can hypnotise people?"

"Only the larger, more intelligent kind," said Billy. "And they can only hypnotise people who are intelligent themselves. So the girls will be all right," he added with a smirk.

Alicia shuffled in her chair as though she often had to put up with this sort of thing. Beatrice looked as though she was going to say something but decided against it. Dr. Drake looked at Billy archly.

"I dare say that a dragon could hypnotise nearly everyone in this room if he chose to," he said.

"Could the knucker—?" began Beatrice, but she was cut off by a tremendous thud that made the whole building shake. We all stood up at once. It sounded as though someone—or something—was trying to smash the wall down.

"Look!" said Alicia. A huge dragon's head appeared at one of the windows. From the size of its head, I guessed that the creature would make the knucker look tiny and would positively dwarf Scorcher. When it saw us, its head started moving against the window as though it were hopping up and down in excitement.

"Jamal's gotten out again," cried Darcy.

"How on earth?" exclaimed Dr. Drake.

We crowded over to one of the other windows and looked out to see Emery and Mademoiselle Gamay trying to deal with a dragon that stood at least twelve feet high. He had two enormous wings at the front and two huge back legs, but no front legs at all.

"Jamal's come to say hello," said Billy with a laugh.

Meanwhile Mademoiselle Gamay was trying to attract the beast's attention with the remains of the roast beef we had eaten for lunch, while Emery held out a large bowl full of glass beads.

"Can't we go and see him?" asked Billy.

"Not now," said Dr. Drake. "There will be plenty of time to see Jamal later. But if you watch, you may learn something. I am sure that Emery and Mademoiselle Gamay have got the situation under control."

It didn't seem like it. The dragon was ignoring both of them. Instead, he was testing the wall with his hind claws and tail, as though he was wondering just what it would take to knock it down. Then he moved back a little and thumped the wall again with his tail. The building shook as though there had been a small earthquake.

"Shouldn't we get outside?" asked Beatrice.

"Not just yet," said Dr. Drake.

Then a rather red-faced Emery managed to get in front of Jamal, distracting him for a moment by placing the bowl of glass beads in front of him.

Jamal looked briefly at the bowl, tossed his head, and then turned to continue his tail thumping.

Mademoiselle Gamay had given up on the remains of the beef and instead had gone to fetch an old penny-farthing bicycle. Suddenly, Emery dashed forward, snatched back the bowl of glass beads, and hopped onto the bicycle. Wobbling a little, he pedalled off as fast as he could towards the forest.

Jamal, noticing that his gift had been taken away from him, now gave Emery his full attention, letting out a roar as he turned his twelve-foot bulk and half flew half ran after Emery, who was whooping with all his might. Soon, both of them had disappeared amongst the trees.

"He's only a baby," said Dr. Drake with a smile. "The glass beads trick usually works. But I do wonder how he keeps on getting out."

"Father's not going to be pleased," said Billy.

Chapter Twelve
DRAGON THEORY

Oft repeated, oft ignored: underestimate the awful
dangers of dragon hypnosis at your gravest peril.
—— Dr. Drake's Dragon Diary, March 1846

D r. Drake said that he needed to go off in case Emery needed help recapturing Jamal, and so lessons ended for the day, but not before he set us some homework to do. Beatrice, Alicia, and I had to study the map on the wall and write short descriptions of all the dragons we found. Billy and Darcy were going to help us with names and descriptions of the species of dragons that they knew. Dr. Drake had also handed them sheets of paper with information about two new dragon species they hadn't studied before. I had soon copied the map into my record book and drawn rough sketches of the dragons on it. I thought I could recognise a knucker, which looked like Weasel; a wyvern, like Jamal; and a European dragon, which looked a bit like an adult Scorcher.

"European dragons live amongst mountains or in sea caves," said Billy. "They grow up to forty-five feet long, breathe fire, and mainly eat cattle, deer, or sheep."

"I haven't actually seen Scorcher breathe fire," I said. "Only smoke."

"That's because he's a baby. It takes them a little while to learn how to do it properly."

"And what's this dragon?" I asked. It was in Australia.

"It's a marsupial dragon," said Billy. "I've never seen one, but according to Dr. Drake, they raise one young at a time in a fiery pouch."

"And they like to box," I said. I remembered what he had told me about the shady dealer from Shadwell Dock.

Soon I had made a list of names and descriptions of the dragons in my record book, and Billy had gone into a corner to read the sheets that Dr. Drake had given him. Beatrice, meanwhile, had gotten together with Alicia and had raced through the map exercise with Darcy. I listened as she started asking him about the other posters on the walls.

"What's that?" asked Beatrice, pointing to a poster that showed a picture of a hat that had diamonds hanging round the rim.

"That's a Back o' Bourke bush hat," said Darcy. "They use them in Australia to attract marsupial dragons. You see, Australian cattle drovers sometimes hang corks round their hats to keep the flies away, but dragonologists use fake diamonds instead."

"What sort of dragon is that?" asked Alicia, going over to Billy and pointing at the sheet he was reading.

Billy immediately swung round so that she couldn't see the sheet.

"It's advanced dragonology," he said. "I don't expect you girls will get to this level for a while. I'll show Daniel, though. He seems to catch on quite quickly."

He winked at me, and I was just about to go over and have a look when Beatrice hissed, "Daniel, that's not fair."

I sighed and sat down again. It did seem a bit unfair.

We went back to the house to find that Dr. Drake and Emery had returned from rounding up Jamal and reinforcing the fence on his compound. They were deep in conversation, and Dr. Drake looked very worried, but they hushed up as soon as we appeared. Emery fetched a leather ball and told us to kick it around between ourselves.

"You'll find out why later," he said. "But it's going to be fun."

That evening, when Billy was talking to Dr. Drake, Darcy came and showed me the sheets of paper he and Billy had been given. There were two dragons on it. One looked a bit like an imp with arms, legs and claws and was the sort of thing you might expect to see on the side of an ancient cathedral. It was called a gargouille. The other was a small, nasty-looking creature that seemed more like an evil crow than a dragon. It was a cockatrice.

"Dr. Drake says that cockatrices are very rare, but that they are among the most dangerous of dragons because they can kill their prey merely by breathing on them. They usually live in Mediterranean mountain forests, but I'm sure Dr. Drake mentioned one that lives in England or Wales somewhere. It's called Bog-Crow. He also said that a few of them migrated to North America. He thinks that it might have been the source for the legend of the *Marie Celeste*—all the passengers and crew were killed by cockatrices, but the dragons got away."

"Let's show Beatrice," I said.

But when we knocked on the door of the girls' dormitory, there was no reply.

I knocked harder, and a voice shouted back, "Sorry. Closed for Q.T.B."

"Beatrice," I hissed. "Do you want to see a cockatrice?"

The door flew open. Inside, the room was already covered with pictures and diagrams of dragons that Beatrice and Alicia had made, and their dragonological record books were open alongside Darwin's *On the Origin of Species*. Beatrice had obviously been teaching Alicia everything she had learned about evolution. Alicia was sitting on the floor beside a large version of the map and some figures of dragons and dragonologists. It seemed as though Beatrice had made up some kind of dragon game.

"What's Q.T.B.?" I asked.

"It's a club," said Beatrice. "No boys allowed."

"All right," I said, "I believe you. But do you want to see this cockatrice?"

Beatrice fetched a piece of paper so that she could copy it all out.

"Do you mind?" she asked Darcy.

"Not at all," he said. "And I'm sure Dr. Drake won't mind either, now that you have done the homework he set."

"Thank you," she said.

While Beatrice copied out the details, I tried to have a look at the game she had invented.

"How do you play?" I asked.

"Sorry," said Beatrice. "Q.T.B. members only."

"But what does it stand for?" I asked.

"Quicker than boys."

And she shut the door.

The following morning we had an introduction to Eastern dragons. We learned that while dragons in the West are often thought of as horrible monsters, in the East, dragons are considered beneficial helpmeets to mankind and are celebrated with dragon dances and dragon boat races.

In the afternoon we learned about a polar cousin of the European dragon known as the frost dragon. We charted the migratory routes of some frost dragons based on sightings by various S.A.S.D. agents. One of the sightings had come from a place in northern India. I wondered if our parents had reported it.

✦ ✦ ✦

The next day Emery and Mademoiselle Gamay taught a class on the life cycle of dragons. Mademoiselle Gamay told us that dragons grow continually through their lives, like snakes and crocodiles, and we spent some time looking at various pictures of dragons and estimating their ages from their sizes. Emery showed us an interesting series of pictures that showed how a dragon embryo develops in the egg.

On the fourth day Dr. Drake brought in to the schoolroom a pile of what he called dragon-tracking paraphernalia. There was a flameproof cloak, which looked like a piece of canvas that had been painted with some sort of flame-retardant paint, a whistle that was supposed to summon dragons, and a pair of binoculars that had a convenient compass set into the handle. After he had let us look at them—cautioning us not under any circumstances to blow the whistle—he pointed to the blackboard, which still had the diagram he had drawn showing how dragons breathe fire.

"Can anyone remember how fire is produced?" he asked.

Beatrice's hand shot up. So did Billy's, but it was a fraction of a second later.

"Well, Beatrice?" said Dr. Drake.

Beatrice smiled. This was obviously Q.T.B. in action.

"The dragon has a special pouch where it puts a piece of flint and a piece of iron something or other."

"Pyrites," said Billy and Dr. Drake at the same time.

"Iron pyrites. It uses them to make a spark, and the spark lights the flammable venom in its fangs."

"Quite correct," said Dr. Drake. "Now I think it is time for a little visit to see Scorcher. But we must be careful." And he looked at me. "Scorcher is quite recovered from his illness now, but you mustn't get too close to him. While he is here, I think we can see how he is learning to produce fire. It is quite remarkable, given that he is so young."

We trooped over to the coal shed, and Dr. Drake, who had brought a lantern, unlocked the door. Being very careful not to open the door very wide, he went in first and soothed Scorcher with the same lullaby I had heard him use before, and then he called us in.

Scorcher was sitting in a corner of the shed, looking rather sleepy. He was no longer in his cage, but instead was sitting atop the strangest pile of things imaginable. There were some rocks and pieces of coal, a lot of shiny silver knives, forks, and spoons, two old plates, and some pieces of broken mirror. Right on the top were a few of the glass beads that Emery had used to distract Jamal.

"This is the closest I could get to mimicking a dragon's lair at short notice," said Dr. Drake. "A baby dragon like Scorcher will still spend most of his time in his mother's lair, eating and growing until he is big enough to start learning to fly."

From what I had seen at Dr. Drake's Dragonalia, Scorcher was already learning to fly, but I didn't say anything. I didn't want to do anything much except look at him.

Dr. Drake took a glass bead from his pocket and showed

it to Scorcher, who immediately perked up and gave a little screech.

"Keep back and watch," he said.

He pocketed the bead, and Scorcher immediately left the top of the pile and hopped over towards us.

"Now," said Dr. Drake. "Fetch!"

He pretended to throw the bead over Scorcher's shoulder.

Scorcher raced back over to where he thought the bead had landed and sniffed for it. When he couldn't find it, he became agitated. Pretty soon I saw him making a sort of strange movement with his jaw, and I guessed he was jiggling about a piece of flint and iron pyrites. Sure enough, when you knew what to look for, you could see the little sparks that he was making. I also saw a wisp of the same cloud of sulphurous smoke I had seen in Dr. Drake's Dragonalia.

Scorcher turned and looked right into my eyes as though asking me what had happened to the shiny thing that Dr. Drake had thrown. I couldn't turn away, and I felt a sudden urge to go over to him. As I started going towards him, someone pulled me back, but I shook the person off. Beatrice shouted, and Scorcher started screeching loudly and flapping his wings. I can't remember anything that happened after that until I came to outside. Beatrice and Dr. Drake were standing over me and the other children were standing nearby, looking worried.

"Will he be all right?" demanded Beatrice. "What happened to him?"

"I'm afraid that Daniel has undergone a small case of dragon hypnosis," said Dr. Drake. "I am sorry. It is quite unprecedented for a dragon as young as Scorcher to hypnotise someone. But he will be all right—I promise."

"What happened?" I asked.

"Daniel," said Dr. Drake gravely, "you must rest. When you have rested, I want you to come and see me in my office. But until then I am going to ask you to let me have your dragon record book. And I am going ask you to stay in another bedroom."

I was devastated. Did this mean I wasn't going to be able to study dragons anymore? But I felt so light-headed, I didn't know what to do, so I let Dr. Drake and Mademoiselle Gamay take me upstairs to a bedroom. I lay down and slept for what felt like three days.

CHAPTER THIRTEEN
MR. TIBBS

A person who has been hypnotised by a dragon should
be made to do a large number of complicated
mathematical sums.

——— DR. DRAKE'S DRAGON DIARY, MARCH 1846

As I slept, I dreamt. At first I dreamt that Beatrice was sitting by my side but that when I turned to look at her, I saw Scorcher instead, baring his teeth at me. I tried searching for the beads that he was looking for, but I couldn't seem to find them. He looked angrier and angrier, and sparks and smoke started coming from his mouth as he leaned over me. Then he turned into Dr. Drake, mopping my brow with a damp cloth. Then Dr. Drake turned into Ignatius Crook, holding up one of the glass beads triumphantly.

"It is mine!" cried Ignatius in my dream. "The Dragon's Eye is mine!" He let out a wicked laugh and disappeared into a dark doorway between the window and the wardrobe.

After he had gone, I tried to get up to warn Dr. Drake, but I felt as though I were lying on a bed made of bits of broken mirror and I daren't move in case I rolled over onto anything sharp.

At last I woke up properly in a cold sweat. I felt ravenously hungry, so I got up and went into the kitchen, where Emery was making some coffee.

"Hello, trooper," he said smiling. "You're a sight for sore eyes. Do you feel up to some soup?"

I nodded glumly.

"You're quite a phenomenon," said Emery. "You know, dragons can't usually hypnotise people until they are fully grown. I don't think Scorcher meant to do it. It just happened."

"Will I be able to carry on studying dragonology?" I asked.

"Don't worry about that," he said. "Have some soup!"

But I *was* worried about it. While I was having my soup, Beatrice came rushing in and gave me a hug.

"I was so frightened, Daniel," she said.

"I'm all right," I said.

After I had finished the soup, we went into the garden. I looked at the rabbits. I thought about Weasel and Jamal and Scorcher. Then I saw a strange carriage, sitting by the side of the house.

"I've got to go and see Dr. Drake," I said.

"I think he's got company," said Beatrice.

"I have to go and see him, though," I said.

When I got to Dr. Drake's study, I had a strong sense of déjà vu. There was a lot of angry shouting coming from inside, and I heard the name Ignatius Crook more than once. *It must be Mr. Tibbs,* I thought. So instead of knocking, I waited outside, where I could hear what was going on. This is what I heard:

"And what about the reports coming from Cornwall about a huge, fiery monster crawling about the farms at night and stealing sheep? Or the stories of travellers scared on the road by an enormous winged serpent flying up and down the east coast of Scotland? The newspapers haven't printed any of these stories yet, but we are having a hard time putting them all down as the ramblings of deluded cranks. It won't be very long before someone puts two and two together and gets 'dragon'!"

That was Mr. Tibbs.

"And I repeat that this has nothing to do with the Secret and Ancient Society. Although it is an extremely worrying development."

That was Dr. Drake.

"Coupled with your having a live and very dangerous dragon right in the heart of London, I would have said that it is rather more than a worrying development!" yelled Mr. Tibbs.

"As I said, from your descriptions, it certainly seems that someone has been up to no good. Has anyone spoken to Ignatius Crook?"

"Of course. It was Ignatius Crook who was kind enough to inform the Minister that your ill-starred experiments in so-called dragon science seemed to have taken a turn for the worse. He was entertaining a lady dragonologist and was taking her to see your shop when he discovered what you were up to."

"You're saying that he came round to see me at six o'clock in the morning," said Dr. Drake. "That hardly seems a very sociable hour to be paying visits. And surely the Minister does not distrust my version of events entirely. Otherwise he would not have sent his son to my summer school, don't you think?"

"I am not entirely privy to the Minister's thoughts, Doctor," said Mr. Tibbs. "But I believe you to be an ambitious man. The Minister and I have had to spend a great deal of time hushing up dragon incidents that involved you in the past. Of course, you always claimed that you were only doing what was necessary in order to protect both humans and dragons. Can you really assure me that you are not seeking those dragonological treasures that Ebenezer Crook and the late Lord Chiddingfold determined should be returned to the safekeeping of the Society of Dragons? You are one of the few men who could discover where they are. You would find their powers extremely useful. Of that I have no doubt."

"And are *you* sure that it is not *Ignatius Crook* who is searching for them?" said Dr. Drake. "As far as I can see, he considers them to be family heirlooms. He was very upset when his father refused to tell him where they were. He feels he has been robbed."

"We all know that Ignatius has made mistakes in the past, but he has sworn to the Minister that his only interest in dragons is theoretical."

"And who is the woman he was with?"

"Her name is Alexandra Gorynytchka. She is a Russian, I believe, and a leading member of the Russian Dragonological Society. She is here on a research trip."

"I think I have met Miss Gorynytchka. What is she researching?"

"I am not sure—dragon diseases or something. In any case, it is beside the point. The Minister wants to know when you are going to release the two dragons you are supposedly looking after. You are sure you are not training them for something? Surely it is time they both went back into the wild. We have heard reports that you are unable to keep Jamal in his compound. I hope that we shall not have to cover up further reports of fiery devastation in the Sussex countryside?"

"I can assure you that I am taking every step to keep Jamal confined," said Dr. Drake. "We check up on him every day, and I shall take him home to North Africa myself the very minute he is able to fly properly."

I was engrossed in this conversation, but suddenly I heard another noise behind me. Someone was coming up the stairs. I quickly knocked on Dr. Drake's door. The voices within went quiet, and the door swung open.

"Why, Daniel," said Dr. Drake, "I am glad to see you looking so well. Mr. Tibbs is just leaving."

Mr. Tibbs looked as red-faced as I remembered from the first meeting.

"Well, I daresay I have said my piece for now," he said. "Just be careful, Drake. I don't want to hear about any more burning barns or missing sheep!"

And with that, he took his hat and left, nodding to Emery, who had come up the stairs and was now standing at the door with a sheaf of papers.

Emery placed the papers on Dr. Drake's desk.

"Thank you, Emery," said Dr. Drake, turning to me. "Now, Daniel, you have had quite a shock with Scorcher. The fault is mine, for I have never come across a case such as this with such a young dragon. Hypnosis can be a dangerous thing unless it is caught early enough. Nevertheless, I am going to administer a fail-safe cure, which you may not like but which will certainly do you good. I want you to forget all about dragons for a while and concentrate on working out the answers to these pages of mathematical sums. When I am satisfied, we shall talk again."

I took the sheaf of papers back to my new room. There were quite literally hundreds of mathematical sums. I didn't like the look of them at all. Suddenly, life at Dr. Drake's was beginning to feel very like boarding school, except that all of the other children were having the most fantastic time learning about dragons, while I was doing sums.

Beatrice came to see me.

"Are you all right?" she said.

"No," I said. "I've got to do about a million sums."

"Dr. Drake says that's the best way to cure someone who has been hypnotised by a dragon," she said.

I told her what I had overheard Mr. Tibbs tell Dr. Drake.

Beatrice was quiet for a moment.

"Don't worry," she said. "I am sure that Dr. Drake has everything under control. When you are better, I will tell you what I have learned in class. After all, Billy needs to learn that girls are—"

"More or less about the same speed as boys?" I said.

"Quicker!" said Beatrice with a laugh.

And she left me to my pages and pages of sums.

CHAPTER FOURTEEN
THE SOCIETY OF DRAGONS

DRACO-RACO-ACODRAC. A powerful word, to be
sure. But what on earth can it possibly mean?
—— DR. DRAKE'S DRAGON DIARY, APRIL 1847

Even though I desperately hated being made to do so
many pages of sums, I was equally desperate for the
cure to be a success, and I went at them as hard as I could. I
think I must have got through about fifteen pencils and ten
erasers. Every evening Dr. Drake would come up to check
my work. By the end of three days, I had could probably
have recited my times tables all the way up to about fifty or
sixty, and my head was so swimming with numbers that I
even started doing sums in my sleep.

Finally I finished a page that ended like this:

$$3.14159 \times 3963.205 \times 3963.205$$
$$2 \times 3.1459 \times 3963.205$$

$$299792458 \times 7926.41$$
$$1.09714 \times 3$$
$$1357911 \times 3.14159$$
$$123456 \div 17$$
$$727218 \div 81$$
$$299792458 \div 14$$

It took me less than twenty minutes, and Dr. Drake finally pronounced himself satisfied that the cure had worked and that I could rejoin the other children. That night after dinner, I took Beatrice aside.

"Dr. Drake says that I'm cured," I said. "But I must be careful not to see Scorcher for a while."

"Thank goodness," said Beatrice. "Billy is not being helpful, to say the least. Darcy is amazing. But Billy seems to think that the classes are all for him, and whenever he knows something that we don't—which obviously he does, because he's studied dragons for longer—he says it's too difficult for girls and won't explain it."

"What have you been studying?" I asked.

"We've been learning about the history of the S.A.S.D.," said Beatrice.

"Can you tell me about it?" I asked.

"Well," said Beatrice, "it all started in about 1281, when King Edward I ordered the extermination of all the dragons in the kingdom. Unfortunately, quite a few knights joined in and things began to look pretty bad for the dragons.

There were some people, however, who tried to help them, including a lady dragonologist named Beatrice Croke."

"You must have been named after her!" I said.

"Perhaps," said Beatrice. "She narrowly avoided being burned as a witch and escaped to Scotland. Before then, most intelligent dragons had been happy sleeping in their lairs. But now they started to seek each other out, and the Society of Dragons was formed. It was only through a great deal of cunning that Beatrice Croke managed to convince them not to burn down London, York, and several other large cities. She helped them to hide the treasures of some of the dead dragons and formed the Secret Society of Dragonologists with her son Daniel. We call it the Secret and Ancient Society because, as far as we know, it is the oldest dragonological society in the world."

"So we _were_ named after them," I exclaimed.

"It seems like it. Anyway, over the years the S.A.S.D. collected twelve special treasures. Although they were made at different times in different countries, each one of them gives the wielder certain powers over dragons. And they were the treasures that Ebenezer Crook returned to the dragons before he died."

"Since Ignatius is Ebenezer's son, I wouldn't be at all surprised if he was searching for them!" I said.

"Yes," said Beatrice. "Dr. Drake's suggestion may have been right."

Beatrice fetched her record book so that I could copy down the list of treasures. This is what I copied:

The Dragonological Treasures of the S.A.S.D.

NOTE: *Most are ineffective without the accompanying charm.*

1. THE TALISMAN OF MASTER MERLIN *An extremely powerful Welsh artefact that has the power to call upon the aid of a mighty dragon—if you know the right words.*

2. SPLATTERFAX *From ancient Russia, this amulet is said to bring down a hail of rocks on its unfortunate victims; legend says that it was brought to England in 1066 by the Norwegian King Harald Hardrada but was lost at the Battle of Stamford Bridge before he could use it.*

3. SAINT PETROC'S CHALICE *An ancient Cornish cup that bears around its rim the ingredients of a sure cure for sick dragons, which must be mixed in the cup itself.*

4. ABRAMELIN'S DRAGON ATTRACTOR *From England, this is an iron ornament in the shape of a hexagon, fitted with a gemstone that can be used to locate particular kinds of dragons.*

5. THE DRAGON'S CLAW *Said to come from China, the claw has various properties and is a powerful ingredient in many different kinds of dragon spells.*

6. THE SPEAR OF SAINT GEORGE *More like an African assegai than a traditional spear, this is one of the few weapons hard and sharp enough to kill a dragon.*

7. A BOX OF DRAGON DUST *Dragon dust is a very rare substance, normally available only in minute quantities. Some of this dust, collected in Austria, dates back to the 1280s; the rest was collected much later.*

8. *LIBER DRACONIS* *A book written in Dragonish by Gildas Magnus and said to have been copied from an original kept in the Reales Alcazares in Seville, Spain. Only a true Dragon Master is allowed to know what it contains.*

9. SAINT GILBERT'S HORN *From Scotland, this horn has the power to summon any nearby dragon. Combined with dragon dust, a powerful taming effect may be obtained that lasts for a number of weeks.*

10. THE DRAGON SCEPTRE *Said to have come from ancient Peru sometime before Columbus discovered America, the sceptre can be used only once to summon an army of dragons, after which it will break into pieces.*

11. A VIAL OF DRAGON'S BLOOD *Like dragon dust, dragon's blood is very rare, and it is forbidden to collect it these days. It is also very dangerous. However, in extremely small doses it can assist in understanding Dragonish. This vial contains blood collected in India.*

12. THE DRAGON'S EYE GEM *Lost for many years, this gem has the power of confirming the status of a true*

*Dragon Master. As such, it must be returned to the
Society of Dragons upon the death of each previous
Dragon Master, and kept until such time as they elect a
new one.*

"What does it mean by the 'accompanying charm'?" I
asked when I had finished copying the list.

"It means you have to use some special words," said
Beatrice.

"What, like magic?" I said.

"Yes, but don't worry. We haven't done any magic. Dr.
Drake says it's not something you should meddle with unless you know a lot about it. He says that lots of dragon
charms use supposedly magic words, but that a proper
dragon scientist should pay more attention to the ingredients and the way the charm works."

"Oh," I said.

"Did you know that dragons have their own language?"

"No," I said.

"It's called Dragonish. Only intelligent dragons speak it.
One of the charms is in Dragonish. Dr. Drake taught it to us.
But you need dragon dust in order for it to work properly."

"What is dragon dust, exactly?" I asked.

"Apparently, when a mother dragon has babies, she
breathes out a sort of calming vapour. It condenses on the
walls of dragon lairs in a silvery sheen and it can be scraped
off—if the dragon will let you."

"And what are the words of the charm?"

Beatrice showed me the place in her record book where she had written down instructions for something that Dr. Drake had called Abramelin's Taming Spell. Apparently it lasted three hours, but you needed three troy ounces of dragon dust, whatever troy ounces were, and you had to put them in a silver dish that had been washed three times in water that had reflected a full moon.

"I suppose most water has reflected a full moon at some stage," I said. The rest of the spell involved casting the dragon dust over a dragon you needed to tame, and saying the following strange words:

Ivàhsi yüduin!
Enimôr taym inspelz!
Boyar ugôner gedit!

"I wonder if *taym* means 'tame,'" I said.

"I don't know," said Beatrice. "Dr. Drake wouldn't provide us with a translation."

The next day, I remembered that I had forgotten to ask Beatrice about the leather ball Emery had given us before I was hypnotised, but I didn't have time to ask her anything before we sat down in the classroom, waiting for Dr. Drake.

"First," said Dr. Drake, "I would like to welcome back Daniel. He has been studying mathematics, which ought to be a field of study embraced by all dragonologists. You never know when the ability to perform a lightning-fast calculation might save your life."

He winked at me and continued, "We have studied some dragonology theory—charms and so forth—which luckily all require ingredients that you do not have and so I am not worried about you trying them out by mistake. Today, I shall just finish telling you about the Society of Dragons and then, after an early lunch, there will be time for a spot of fieldwork.

"I will start off by pointing out that while there are various dragonological societies around the world, what I am telling you relates to the societies that were set up in the British Isles in the Middle Ages. As you know, the Society of Dragons was first formed in response to King Edward I's command that dragons be exterminated. The society was a haphazard affair at first, but now there are always seven wise dragons that act as the chief members of the society. They meet every seven years in order to discuss any matters of interest to them. And while an experienced dragonologist like myself may know some of these important dragons and suspect that they are members, the actual composition of the Society of Dragons is a secret known only to the Dragon Master himself.

"Chief among the members of the Society of Dragons is an extremely wise, extremely ancient dragon called the Guardian. Her lair is the most secret of all, because it contains the remains of many hoards that were collected during the last great dragon slaying. Because dragons rightly distrust humans, the only person who has a right to make representations and suggestions to the members of the Society of Dragons on behalf of mankind is the Dragon Master of the Secret and Ancient Society of Dragonologists. This has resolved conflicts and helped both humans and dragons on many occasions. Because of the respect he is accorded among all dragons, the Dragon Master needs some sign of authority. That sign is the Dragon's Eye gem. It supposedly belonged to the magician Merlin, whom many consider the founding father of Western dragonology. When exposed to dragon fire—but only to dragon fire—an image can be fixed within the gem so it is the only image the gem will reflect.

"When the Society of Dragons elects a new Dragon Master—almost always respecting the wishes of the previous one—the Guardian uses her flame to burn his or her image into the Dragon's Eye and presents it to the new Dragon Master. When there is no Dragon Master, then the Dragon's Eye is returned to the Guardian. This situation has been rare, but there has been at least one period before now when there was no Dragon Master. During the reign of Queen Elizabeth I, the gem, along with contact with the Society of Dragons, was very nearly thought to be lost. Now, are there any questions?"

"If the Dragon's Eye can only be awarded by the Society

of Dragons, why would anyone but a Dragon Master search for it?" I asked.

"Well," said Dr. Drake with a twinkle in his eye, "there are two reasons. First, someone might feel that, as their family had been Dragon Masters for more than two hundred years, that they had a hereditary right to it. Second, possessing it would give considerable power over dragons that were not among the seven members of the Society. For a short time they would believe the person was the Dragon Master. This could lead to all sorts of complications. As far as I know, the fire of any adult European dragon would do to fix a reflection in the gem. It does not have to come from the Guardian."

"Do you know where it is?" asked Billy.

"I do not know exactly where it is. There are various notes in my own record book—which I call my Dragon Diary—that could perhaps help me to find it, but I am afraid that unless I am invited by the dragons themselves, or the gem falls under threat, then I, for one, would not be so foolhardy as to go looking for it."

"Might anyone else be able to find it?" said Beatrice.

"Without spending a great deal of time studying dragons, or without the information in my diary, I very much doubt it. But I think you have learned enough about the Society of Dragons for now. We have some rather more exciting things to do after lunch than talk about dragons. We are going to meet Jamal."

CHAPTER FIFTEEN
JAMAL

Young dragons learn to fly by flapping their wings and
leaping about. If at first you don't succeed,
fly, fly again!
—— DR. DRAKE'S DRAGON DIARY, MARCH 1849

After lunch, Dr. Drake and Emery met us at the front of his house.

"Is everyone ready to go?" asked Dr. Drake.

"Are you sure that it will be safe for Daniel?" asked Beatrice.

"I'm quite sure," said Dr. Drake. "While Scorcher seems rather out of the ordinary, quite possibly as a result of the disease he was suffering from, Jamal is a perfectly normal young wyvern, and there is absolutely no danger of being hypnotised by him. The time will soon come when I must take him home to Africa. However, he is a playful fellow, and I think he will be quite glad of a visit. In any case, as he seems to be escaping from his compound quite a lot, I think it is a good idea if we all check up on him from time to time. It will give Darcy a break, anyway."

I suddenly realised what Darcy's mysterious disappearances had been about—he had been going to check up on Jamal all along.

Dr. Drake turned to Emery and said, "Have you got the ball?"

Emery showed it to him, and Dr. Drake then took an apple out of his pocket and cut it in half.

"Jamal is learning to fly," he said. "He jumps and leaps and moves his wings about in order to exercise them. He is very well fed, which makes him friendly, and he also has a lair, which he protects at all costs. Now, it is a little-known fact that, while dragons love lettuce, they hate apples with a vengeance because they give them stomachaches. So, it naturally follows that Jamal will not want anything that smells of apple in his lair."

And at that he took the cut piece of apple and rubbed it all over the leather ball.

"Your job today is to kick this ball past Jamal and into his lair. I don't think you will be able to succeed. But since it's a game, I need someone to go on Jamal's team."

This time Billy's hand shot up a fraction of a second before Beatrice's.

"All right, then," said Dr. Drake.

We trooped through the forest and soon arrived at the fence, which I now knew to be protecting Jamal's compound.

It showed signs of having been repaired several times. Emery took us round through a dark clump of pines to a small gate.

Emery unlocked it, and we went through.

Almost as soon as we were inside, there was a rustling amongst the bushes and Jamal ran forwards to meet us. Then he bounded away, flapping his wings as though he were showing off.

"That's right, Jamal," said Dr. Drake with a laugh. "Lead the children to your lair."

It wasn't hard to find Jamal's lair. There was a huge pile of bones outside, and I thought that Dr. Drake must have been keeping at least ten butchers in business with all the feeding he needed to do. Like Weasel's den, Jamal's lair was dug into the sand, but it was dug into a tall bank and it looked much more like a cave mouth than a simple hole.

"Now," said Dr. Drake, "show Jamal the ball."

Emery took the ball and showed it to Jamal. The dragon came over and sniffed it. He looked puzzled for a moment. Then he leapt back towards his lair and stood in the entrance, looking at us warily.

"Right," said Dr. Drake as Emery placed the ball on the ground. "Billy, if you go and join Jamal and kick the ball away, he will realise that you want to help him. You other four—your goalmouth is between those two large pines over there."

This was amazing. Dr. Drake was actually going to get us to play dragon football.

"Who's going in our goal?" I said.

"I will," said Alicia. "I'm afraid I'm not very good at kicking balls."

But she had hardly started back for the two trees, when Billy came running towards her and kicked the ball into our goal.

"Easy!" he said.

Alicia trudged through the undergrowth, fetched the ball and threw it back into the middle, where it landed near Billy's feet.

"We haven't started yet," said Darcy.

"Then we'll start—now!" shouted Billy. And he began dribbling the ball with his foot. Beatrice tried to tackle him, but he simply shoved her out of the way.

"That's not fair," said Beatrice.

But by now *I* was trying to tackle Billy. *He isn't going to shove me,* I thought.

Unfortunately, he didn't need to. He got past me in three swift steps and advanced on Darcy. He looked up, and then kicked the ball hard, but not at the goalmouth. It bounced off Darcy's head, knocking his spectacles flying.

"Sorry!" said Billy.

Darcy had to scramble for his glasses to make sure they weren't trodden on while Billy dribbled the ball up to his sister, who was making the most half-hearted goal-keeping effort I have ever seen. I think she was afraid that the ball might sting if it hit her.

Billy coolly passed the ball into the goal behind her.

"Dragons two, Dragonologists nil!" he shouted, running back towards Jamal's lair.

Alicia trudged off to retrieve the ball again.

Beatrice looked over at Dr. Drake.

"It's not fair," she said. "We're supposed to be seeing how Jamal guards his lair."

"Then I expect you need a plan," said Dr. Drake.

When Alicia had got the ball back again, Beatrice drew us together.

"Team talk!" she said. "There are four of us and two of them. All we need to do is get the ball off Billy. Let's go!"

Alicia threw the ball out carefully, so that it landed between Billy and Beatrice. Billy ran towards it, looking as though he was going to knock Beatrice out of the way again. This time, though, she stepped out of the way at the last minute and knocked the ball sideways. Darcy then ran in and knocked it over to where I was. I dribbled the ball towards Jamal's lair as fast as I could. Billy was running towards me, but he was too far away.

"Come on!" called Beatrice. "Score!"

I looked up. Jamal had started bobbing and weaving in the mouth of his lair, all the time keeping his eye on the ball. I didn't feel entirely confident about kicking the ball past him, but I got in a pretty good shot, up towards the top right-hand corner of the lair mouth.

Jamal, however, simply turned and, using his tail, flicked the ball away as though it were the easiest thing in the world.

Billy was waiting. The ball landed at his feet, and he immediately began to sprint with it. He went past Darcy, and then myself, and then he was bearing down on Beatrice like a runaway train.

"Dodge me!" he cried.

But Beatrice didn't dodge him. She slid out her foot and managed to punt the ball away back towards Alicia.

Billy looked down at his feet in surprise.

"How did you do that?" he said.

But he didn't have any time to think about it, because Alicia had passed the ball out to Darcy, who had passed it to Beatrice, who passed it to me. I dribbled the ball up the field, but this time I wasn't quick enough. Billy was upon me, and even Jamal had come out of his lair mouth towards me.

"Quickly!" shouted Beatrice.

So I passed the ball back to her just at the last moment. Jamal leapt back to protect his lair, and Billy turned so fast that he nearly tripped over his own feet. Beatrice kept her eye on the ball. Although Billy was thundering towards her, she ignored him and, concentrating on Jamal, passed the ball quickly from one foot to the other. Suddenly, just as Billy was about to tackle her, she feinted as though she were going to kick the ball high over Jamal's head then passed it between his legs instead. Billy made contact, and as Beatrice and Billy fell over in a heap, Jamal, taken in by Beatrice's feint, leapt up so energetically and waved his wings so vigorously, that he suddenly found himself semi-airborne and did not get back down to stop the ball in time. But he looked pretty pleased with himself anyway.

"Goal!" cried Emery.

"A good feint!" cried Dr. Drake.

"He flew!" I cried.

"What happened?" asked Billy as Beatrice helped him up.

"We scored!" said Beatrice, laughing.

My sister really is amazing at times.

We didn't get past Jamal again, partly because he was more wary of Beatrice and partly because the third time the ball landed near him, he grabbed it between his feet and, flapping his wings vigorously, took it up into a tree and lodged it between two branches. Although we threw sticks, it wouldn't come down. Jamal looked very pleased with himself. When the ball had been lost, he flapped his wings more than ever, looking at them proudly.

"Soon he will be flying for real!" said Dr. Drake. "But for now, we had best return home."

While the others set off, I lingered for a few minutes to watch Jamal, who came to the gate to see us go. Soon the others had disappeared, and I hurried along the path to catch up with them. But I had only gone a few hundred yards when I heard a loud cracking noise behind me. It sounded like splintering wood. Had someone returned to Jamal's compound? I turned to go back and saw a woman stepping out from behind a tree. She was very tall and had pale skin and jet-black hair. She was dressed in a large black cape, high riding boots, and a very large, black hat. She was beautiful. Suddenly, there was a rustling noise in the trees. It was Jamal. He ran past us through the forest at top speed.

I opened my mouth to cry out. The woman smiled, but it was not a nice smile. Putting her finger to her lips, as though urging me to be quiet, she started coming towards me. I froze. I could hear distant shouts up ahead. The woman turned and vanished among the trees. I started to run. I felt that I needed to warn Dr. Drake at all costs.

When I reached the house, it was clear the others had seen Jamal, too.

"You didn't open the gate, did you?" asked Billy.

"Why would I do that?" I said.

I started to explain about the woman I had seen, but Dr. Drake raised his hand and cut me off.

"It is absolutely essential that Jamal is recaptured at once," he said. "I am afraid that I will have to think of somewhere rather safer to keep him than his compound. But first we must find him. All of you, I want you to spread out and use the dragon tracking skills you have learned to try and find him as quickly as possible. But do be careful not to disturb Weasel. Emery, you take the south part of the forest with Alicia. Mademoiselle Gamay, you take the north with Billy and Darcy. Daniel and Beatrice, we will take the west side. Come with me."

I opened my mouth to speak, but Dr. Drake said, "This is

not the time for questions, Daniel. It is a very serious situation."

"It's not a questi—" I began.

"Hush!" he said, cupping his ear to listen as carefully as he could to the forest sounds.

"But—" I said.

"But nothing!" he said. He listened again and then let out a strange sort of keening cry. When nothing happened, he waited a few minutes more and then did it again. This time, he must have thought he had heard something, for he bounded away off the path and up a steep slope, where Beatrice and I had a hard time keeping up. In fact, it took us about another quarter of a mile before we were able to catch up with him again as he paused near a clump of pines.

This time I was determined.

"Dr. Drake," I panted, pointing in what I thought was the direction of Jamal's compound.

"What, Daniel? Have you found some signs?"

"No," I said. "I saw a woman."

"Where?" he asked.

"At Jamal's compound," I said. "I'm sure I heard her breaking the fence."

Dr. Drake looked exasperated.

"Why on earth didn't you say so?" he said.

"I tried to!" I said.

"What did she look like?" he said.

I told him.

A look of understanding suddenly crossed Dr. Drake's features.

"It is Alexandra Gorynytchka," he exclaimed. "We must return to the house at once. There isn't a moment to lose!"

A terrible sight awaited us when we got to Dr. Drake's house. The front door had been wrenched off its hinges, and as we ran up the hall towards Dr. Drake's study, I saw that the parlour had been rifled and that the picture frames were all hanging at odd angles, as though someone had been looking behind them.

But things were even worse in Dr. Drake's study. For there, everything had been turned upside down. Papers lay everywhere, pots of ink were spilt on the floor, books had been thrown off shelves, and every drawer and cupboard had been opened, and their contents pulled out. Whatever had happened, it had certainly happened in a hurry.

"Have they taken anything valuable?" exclaimed Beatrice as we stood staring at the sight of Dr. Drake dismally surveying the wreckage.

"Yes," said Dr. Drake. "I am afraid to say that they have taken the most valuable thing I owned. My dragon diary is missing."

CHAPTER SIXTEEN
THE DRAGON DIARY

The dragonological record book is without doubt the
most useful tool of the scientific dragonologist. Keep
a dragon diary, and one day it may keep you!
—— DR. DRAKE'S DRAGON DIARY, AUGUST 1849

I do not think I have ever seen Dr. Drake angrier than at
that moment. His dragon diary contained all of the
records that he had made during his entire life. For many
people, these records would have seemed to be nothing
more than fantastical ramblings, but for someone who was
interested in dragons, they were a priceless resource.

"Don't you have a copy?" I asked.

"A copy?" he said. "I'm afraid not. I only wish that I had
taken the trouble to hide my dragon diary more securely,
but it is difficult. I refer to it on a daily basis."

Suddenly, Dr. Drake broke off. He glanced out the
window.

Beatrice and I had the same thought.

"Scorcher!" we cried.

We followed Dr. Drake as he ran outside to the coal shed. But it too had been broken into. The baby dragon was gone.

Dr. Drake hung his head.

"I have failed him," he said.

As we arrived back at the house, he bent down and picked up a letter that had been left on the mat. There was another letter propped up on a chair outside Dr. Drake's study.

Dr. Drake opened the first letter. After reading it he said, "It is from your uncle Algernon," he said. "It seems that Ignatius Crook has written to him, explaining that he ought to know who is looking after you both. Apparently your parents do not know the whole truth about me, which is why Ignatius has written to your uncle to warn him that I am a monster who teaches children dangerous nonsense about dragons. Algernon says that he is coming to pick you both up the day after tomorrow and that he will come back with a policeman if I do not give you up immediately."

"Why would Uncle Algernon believe Ignatius Crook?" I asked. I couldn't imagine anything worse than going to stay with Uncle Algernon now that we had learned so much dragonology.

"Your uncle will not have needed much persuading," said Dr. Drake. "Your parents are sure to have talked to him about me, and I am sure that he thinks I am a dangerous lunatic. In some ways, I am surprised he has not tried to come and rescue you before."

"What about the other letter?" asked Beatrice.

"Ah, yes," said Dr. Drake. "The other letter."

Surprisingly, Dr. Drake gave it to us so that we could read it for ourselves.

My dear Ernest,

As you have sought fit to deprive me of knowledge of the location of a large part of my inheritance, I have had to take matters into my own hands. I have therefore been forced to borrow some of your papers. These, I am sure, will give me all the clues I need in order to locate the missing heirlooms. In the meantime I expect that Algernon Green will be along to pick up the Cook children any day now. I suggested that he bring along a policeman or two, just in case. As you know, I am a dear friend of their parents, and it will be pleasing to know they are safely out of your hands. I might even pay them a little visit if I have the time. As for that poor animal you kept locked in your coal shed, I took pity on it and decided that since you seem to have cured it, it might come in handy.

Yours sincerely,
Ignatius Crook

P.S. By the way, I ought to tell you that at least one of the family treasures has now been restored to me. I think that will come in handy, too!

"Can't you just take this to the police?" asked Beatrice when she had finished reading it.

"Dear me, no," said Dr. Drake. "Can you imagine my explaining Scorcher to them? Or the fact that I am a dragonologist?"

"But why is Ignatius bothered about us?" I asked.

"I am afraid," said Dr. Drake, "that it is time I told you a few things that have an important bearing on your lives. As you know, Ignatius's father was Ebenezer Crook. He was the last Dragon Master, and he died seven years ago. Before he died, he decided that he could trust no one to look after the ancient treasures of the Secret and Ancient Society. He had come to believe that dragons should be left alone and that no good would come of people interfering with them. So he placed the treasures in the hands of the Society of Dragons for safekeeping, refusing to tell anyone where they were hidden or which dragons were looking after them. As the position of Dragon Master had been in the Crook family for so long, Ignatius seemed to think that the position had become hereditary and that his father had somehow disinherited him. Although I was wary of Ignatius, I felt that our world, with all its science and discoveries, had changed, and I did not agree with my old tutor on the subject of dragon science. Indeed, I firmly believed then as I believe now that a proper understanding of dragonology is the only way for us to ensure that dragons and humans are able to live side by side. I continued to teach a class at my little shop near the

Seven Dials. Ignatius came to me, asking to be taught, and for the sake of his father, I took him on.

"Of course, I did not know where the treasures had been hidden, but over the course of a few years, as I have made contact with a good many dragons—particularly in the British Isles—I began to form an idea of how they might be found. I respected Ebenezer's wishes enough to leave them where they were, but I did make a record of my findings, I am afraid to say, in my dragon diary.

"Shortly after Ebenezer's death, in fact, only about a week after his funeral, I was called to investigate a dragon sighting in West Chiltington. While I was away, your father found Ignatius Crook in my office. He had made a copy of my keys and was busy writing out portions of my dragon diary. At first, Ignatius was very nice to him, promising him great things if he would help him to become Dragon Master. But your father refused all of Ignatius's offers and told me immediately what had happened. Ignatius was furious and vowed revenge. Shortly after that, your father fell sick with a mysterious illness that the doctors said was due to some kind of food poisoning."

"Poisoning!" exclaimed Beatrice. "Couldn't you help him?"

"Indeed I could. That was when I came to stay with you. With the proper care from my own doctor, he recovered entirely. I nearly managed to catch up with Ignatius Crook in Scotland. He had managed to upset one dragon pretty badly, and the creature was causing considerable devastation. It took me ages to calm it down. But before I could find Ignatius, he disappeared abroad. You see it was then that he stole the treasure he refers to in his letter. He is in possession of Saint Gilbert's horn. The next treasure that he will seek out is the box of dragon dust. Combined with Saint Gilbert's horn, Ignatius will find that he can bend even the mightiest dragons to his will. If he manages to find the Dragon's Eye, he will then have the fire he needs in order to fix his reflection in it and become, to all intents and purposes, the Dragon Master."

"But why hasn't Ignatius tried to steal your diary before now?" I asked.

"His understanding of dragonology was always rather superficial. I am sure that he went abroad to try and recruit some help. I wonder if it will be the sort of help that he was expecting."

"And what about our parents?" asked Beatrice. "Why did they go to India?"

"Your parents are dragonologists," replied Dr. Drake. "As such, they are sworn to conserve and protect dragons wherever they may be, even if it means they must send their children to boarding school. Before he died, Ebenezer Crook received a communication from the Maharawal of Jaisalmer, in northern India. In it, the Maharawal asked for help investigating a strange sickness that had begun to afflict a kind of dragon called a naga in the Thar Desert. Although by now he was reluctant to interfere with dragon affairs, Ebenezer owed the Maharawal a favour, and so he gave this mission to your parents on the condition that they wait until you were old enough to go to school."

"But weren't they in danger from Ignatius?" said Beatrice.

"No," said Dr. Drake. "In fact Ignatius did turn up in Jaisalmer, but the Maharawal is a good friend of mine, and his soldiers soon made it clear that it would be too dangerous for him to stay there. I have a feeling that it must have been shortly after that that he met Alexandra Gorynytchka. She is a Russian dragonologist. Her reputation is excellent. She must have agreed to help teach Ignatius the things that he needed to know. But why she has come here and why the concerns of British dragonologists have anything to do with her, I do not know."

Beatrice thought for a moment.

"It seems that the key to all of this is the Dragon's Eye," she said. "Do you have any idea at all where it might be?"

"Well, my diary does contain a note about it from Ebenezer. I only kept the note in case there was some sort of clue on it. But I am sure there wasn't, because I tried everything— invisible ink, codes, ciphers, and all to no avail."

"What did the note say?" I asked.

"Nothing much. It is easy to remember. It said:

My dear Ernest,

I must be brief for I have but hours to live. I fear that I judged you too harshly. I am now convinced that you, indeed, are our best hope. I was blind. Forgive me. I have no

time to make amends. I cannot write openly, nor is there
any friend in whom I can confide. I must take the secret of
the Dragon's Eye to my grave.

> *Yours in dragonology,*
> *Ebenezer Crook."*

"Oh," said Beatrice. "And do you know where his grave
is, then?"

CHAPTER SEVENTEEN
THE *SEA SNAKE*

Although sea serpents share certain features with
dragons —— their ferocity, enormous size, terrifying
aspect, and so on —— they are not remotely related.
—— DR. DRAKE'S DRAGON DIARY, FEBRUARY 1850

By now I could hear the sounds of the others returning.
There were exclamations of shock and surprise as they
beheld the damage.

Dr. Drake looked very serious as he explained the situation to them. "The Secret and Ancient Society of Dragonologists is facing a very great threat," he said.

He mopped his brow before continuing.

"Billy and Alicia, tomorrow morning I must send you
home to your father with Mademoiselle Gamay. I am going
to let you have a letter for Lord Chiddingfold, and I would
be grateful if you could give it to him directly, rather than
through Mr. Tibbs. Emery, I would like you and Darcy to

stay here. There are repairs that must be made to the house, and I need you to keep an eye on Jamal. As for Daniel and Beatrice, I have decided that it is too dangerous for them to stay with their uncle Algernon. Therefore I am going to ask them to come with me."

At that, we looked at each other.

"Will you come?" asked Dr. Drake. "I would be glad of your assistance, at any rate."

"I don't see that we can do anything else," said Beatrice.

I agreed. I felt that if we would be safe with anyone, it would be with Dr. Drake. On our own, or in the company of people like Uncle Algernon, who wouldn't understand the danger, we would be in much greater peril.

Although it was the evening, Dr. Drake decided that we should leave immediately. We would stay overnight in Horsham and catch the first available train to Portsmouth. From there, we would travel by boat to Cornwall, to the grave of the last Dragon Master and, we hoped, to some clues about the location of the Dragon's Eye. Soon Beatrice and I had packed our things and were ready to leave.

"Some people have all the luck," said Billy.

"You call this luck?" said Beatrice incredulously. "To have our lives threatened, and all because your father and Mr. Tibbs don't know how dangerous Ignatius Crook is and chose to believe him rather than Dr. Drake?"

"They won't believe Ignatius anymore, when we tell them what happened," said Alicia.

"Good luck," said Darcy. "If you get separated from Dr. Drake, make your way back here."

Soon a carriage had arrived.

"Never forget Q.T.B.!" said Beatrice to Alicia before leaving. "Tell your friends. Spread the word: Quicker than boys!"

Billy smirked.

"Good luck," he said.

We all solemnly shook hands, then Beatrice and I said good-bye to Emery and Mademoiselle Gamay and got into the carriage with Dr. Drake.

We soon arrived in Horsham. The next morning, Dr. Drake bought us tickets for the Portsmouth train.

"Isn't it much simpler just to take a train to Cornwall?" I asked.

"Indeed," said Dr. Drake. "But you will see that I have very good reasons for taking a ship there. Before we go to Bodmin, I need to try and find the dragon dust."

And he would say no more, except to warn us that Mr. Lubber, who was his agent in Portsmouth, knew nothing of dragons and that we must keep the reasons for our journey secret.

When reached Portsmouth Harbour, Dr. Drake took us down to the harbourmaster's office, where we waited while Mr. Lubber was sent for.

When he arrived, he seemed to be in very much of a fluster.

"If only you had contacted me in advance," he exclaimed.

"Is the *Hydra* not ready, then?" asked Dr. Drake. The *Hydra,* Dr. Drake had told us, was a small ship—more like a large yacht—that belonged to the S.A.S.D. and was sometimes used for scientific investigations. But the *Hydra* was not only not ready; it was not there at all. Mr. Lubber explained that it had been taken the evening before by a man, "who had your own papers, sir, with your own badge and signature and everything. He had a woman with him and he was in a terrible hurry. He didn't even wait for the crew to show up, but said that he had his own. I didn't like the look of them much when I saw them, I can tell you."

"Hmm," said Dr. Drake, frowning. "Is there another boat or yacht we can hire at short notice?"

"There is one other boat I could suggest," said Mr. Lubber, "I fear you will not like it, or its captain, very much and nor do I. It is called the *Sea Snake.*"

"Then let us go and see this captain," said Dr. Drake. "In case you had not noticed, I am in somewhat of a hurry myself."

We went down to the waterfront, where the masts of so many ships—frigates, yachts, liners, cargo ships, fishing vessels, and many others—was certainly a sight worth seeing. It did not take us long to find the captain—whose name was Hezekiah—aboard a dirty sloop that was crewed by some of the crabbiest-looking sailors I had ever seen.

"Cornwall, is it? So this is what we're reduced to," said Captain Hezekiah when Dr. Drake explained that he would like to hire the boat for a "pleasure trip."

"I'm sure you'll not get much pleasure aboard the *Sea Snake,*" said the captain. "Why, the quarters have nearly all been converted to take cargo. But as you are in such a hurry, then if you can see your way to paying this sum. . . ."

Here he showed Dr. Drake a slip of paper, at which Dr. Drake raised his eyebrows, but then shrugged and nodded, saying. "As long as you have at least one cabin fit for a young lady, Captain, then needs must. Mr. Lubber, would you do the honours?"

Mr. Lubber went off to fetch some money and to get a man to bring up our luggage. Dr. Drake turned to us: "Now I would much rather have had you aboard the *Hydra,* but since the trip will only take a couple of days, I think we will manage. But you must take care, of course, not to talk to the crew at all about our trip, and you must not mind anything that you see on the voyage." And, with that, he stepped aboard.

It did not take long for us to install ourselves on the *Sea Snake.* Captain Hezekiah rather reluctantly gave up his cabin for Beatrice, while Dr. Drake and I made do with two hammocks out by the galley. But for some reason, the weather or tides were all wrong, and we could not leave until the following morning.

By then, even though we had not actually been to sea, Beatrice was looking pretty green. When we sailed out of Portsmouth Harbour, she soon took to her cabin, where she stayed for most of the voyage.

I was very excited to be on a ship—however dirty and

untidy—and I managed to ignore the crew, who mostly seemed to spend their time lazing about or checking to see whether the sun had gone down over the yardarm. Meanwhile, Dr. Drake spent a good deal of time with me, explaining the names of all the different sea birds that flew above us, pointing out a school of dolphins, and teaching me the names of all the promontories and lighthouses we could see along the south coast. At about four o'clock in the afternoon, just as we were about to come into sight of Portland, a storm began to blow up and we had to head farther out to sea. But the storm did not last long, and as the light faded, I was just beginning to think about taking to my hammock for a second night, when Dr. Drake drew me to one side.

"Daniel, there is something I want to show you," he said. "It is the reason that I have come to Cornwall by sea. I would have shown it to Beatrice as well, but she is still sleeping off her seasickness."

"Does it have something to do with dragon dust?" I asked.

"Indeed," said Dr. Drake. "But we must be very careful not to let the sailors see what we are up to or things could turn out badly. Meet me by the starboard bow at midnight."

"All right," I said. "But isn't there a chance Ignatius may have found the dragon dust first?"

"There's a chance," said Dr. Drake. "But fortunately my diary gives only very general clues as to its location. With any luck, it will take Ignatius quite some time to find the right spot."

At ten minutes before midnight, as I waited for Dr. Drake, I looked towards the distant shore. Since it was a clear night, I could see enough to make out that it was mainly made up of rocky cliffs dotted with small sandy bays. There was the occasional light from a house at the top, a distant lighthouse away to the left, and another light that seemed to be was moving slowly between the *Sea Snake* and the cliffs. It was not very bright, and I wondered if it was the light from another boat.

"I don't think the sailors can see us from here," whispered Dr. Drake when he arrived, looking around him to see if we were being spied on. "We have passed Plymouth and are quite near a town called St. Austell. Very few people know this, but it was not just Sir Francis Drake's fire ships and terrible weather that helped defeat the Spanish Armada when they tried to invade England, you know. Watch."

And before my wondering eyes, he took out a small packet of powder.

"This," he said, "is serpent bait. Ignatius didn't have time to find it at my house. It is very rare, but it is not magical. It merely consists of the powdered horn of a narwhal, mixed with powdered bone from a whale and a leopard seal, and the dried tentacle of a giant squid. These creatures are the chief prey of the beast I am about to try to attract, which has a very good sense of smell."

At that, he leaned over the rail and sprinkled the powder onto the surface of the sea, whispering:

"Serpent of the briny deep,
If thou wake or if thou sleep,
Stir thyself and come to me,
Serpent, serpent of the sea!"

For a while nothing happened, but then as I looked far out, I saw a movement on the surface of the sea. At first it just seemed to be eddies on the water, reflected under the bright light of the moon. But soon the eddies grew bigger and bigger as though they were being made by some huge beast. Indeed, within moments a monstrous grey snakelike head with huge spines on the top reared out of the water. It looked directly at Dr. Drake, who signalled to it by covering his face with his hands, then bunching them into fists, with the index fingers pointing up.

"This is the serpent sign," he said.

Finally, he leaned over the rail and whispered something to the serpent in a language I could not understand. And what happened next was quite amazing. The serpent disappeared beneath the waves and, after a short time, returned with a small box in its mouth, holding it as gently as a mother dragon holds a chick. Then it reached the box up to Dr. Drake, who spoke to it again.

"This," said Dr. Drake, showing me the box, "is the box of dragon dust. I have been friendly with that serpent for a good many years, and I was with Ebenezer when he consigned his last quantity of dragon dust to its care."

"Can it speak English?" I said.

"Not exactly," said Dr. Drake. "But it can understand some Dragonish. If you like, it will tell you its name. Lean over the rail, and say, '*Ivúwan tünomineh milseh yít.*'"

I leaned over the rail and said the words.

"Quietly, Daniel!" whispered Dr. Drake. "And don't forget to write this down in your record book when you get home. Now, can you see what the serpent is trying to tell us?"

And as I looked, I could see that the swirls seemed to be forming into letters.

"First there's an *L,*" said Dr. Drake.

"Yes, and is that an *E*?" I asked.

"It is, and then a *V.*"

"And then another *L*!" I cried.

"No, no wait. It is not an *L* but an *I*!" said Dr. Drake.

"Yes," I said, "And the next letter seems to be an *A.*"

But we could look no longer, for suddenly a lantern shone behind us and a voice cried, "Captain Hezekiah! They are summoning the sea worm! They are witches! They have called Leviathan!"

We turned and found that most of the crew had sneaked up on us, brandishing all sorts of knives and pistols.

"I am sorry, Daniel," said Dr. Drake. "I rather fear that the crew is unhappy with us."

"Indeed," said Captain Hezekiah, arriving with Beatrice, whom he had pulled from her cabin, and who had turned from looking sleepy, angry, and indignant to looking terrified in an instant.

"Foolish man," said Hezekiah. "Raising monsters! That is bad luck in any sailor's book." He turned to the rest of the crew. "We were right to be suspicious, but now we see that it was for the wrong reasons. We thought that this man had come aboard to investigate those cargoes we bring ashore free of taxes. Smuggling, they call it. Bah! But this is much worse. He is a sorcerer!" Then, shoving Beatrice towards us, where she clung to Dr. Drake, he cried, "Come on, lads. If they can raise a worm, it's time we raised an old custom. Make them walk the plank, and it will be grog all round! But first I shall take that box. Who knows what sum it will bring or what is inside?" And he grabbed Ebenezer's box from Dr. Drake and took it inside.

A plank was swiftly lashed to the foredeck under the rails, and we were made to walk out onto it. When I reached the end, I looked down at the ocean beneath me. Then I looked back at the smugglers with their sharp knives. I heard a splash. Dr. Drake had jumped in. Beatrice and I followed him, hitting the water together. As I reached the surface, I saw that Captain Hezekiah had returned. He didn't look very happy.

"Fools!" he cried. "Idiots! You should have tied their arms. They will swim away. Fetch the harpoons!"

CHAPTER EIGHTEEN
THE BUCCA HOLE

What can be more terrifying to a poor miner than to
hear the dreadful knocking of the bucca, denizen of
deep mines and forgotten caves?

—— DR. DRAKE'S DRAGON DIARY, FEBRUARY 1850

Even though our situation was pretty desperate, to see
poor Dr. Drake floundering and flailing about with his
arms as he tried to swim lightened the gravity of the whole
scene somewhat and probably saved his life. For between
laughing and being unable to aim accurately at Dr. Drake as
he zigged and zagged away from the boat in the darkness,
Hezekiah and his crew of would-be pirates missed shot after
shot. Between each shot, they needed to haul the ramshackle
harpoon they had erected back in on its line. Meanwhile,
Beatrice and I, who could both swim very well, had found a
piece of driftwood and were kicking gamely towards the
shore.

Still, the crew of the *Sea Snake* kept firing and turning the
boat back towards us again and again. No doubt they would

have scored an ace eventually had we not had another stroke of luck. For at that moment the sea serpent rose in front of the ship, taking a harpoon shot that was headed straight for Dr. Drake. The sea serpent shook with rage. Captain Hezekiah grabbed the rope, pulled the harpoon back in on its line, and took careful aim. This time, he was aiming directly at me.

"Good riddance!" he shouted.

But before Captain Hezekiah could release the harpoon, I felt something wet and rubbery around my waist. It was the tip of the sea serpent's tail. It lifted me high out of the water in a huge arc and deposited me on the beach. Then Beatrice was lifted up and set down next to me.

Finally the sea serpent turned to where Dr. Drake had been trying to swim, but he was nowhere to be seen. The serpent's tail disappeared under the water for a moment, then reappeared, gripping Dr. Drake tightly around his waist, and deposited him, spluttering and choking, on the shore.

Now the sea serpent turned its full attention to the ship. The crew stopped firing as Captain Hezekiah ordered them to pile on all the sail they could, but they didn't stand a hope of outrunning the monster. My last view of the *Sea Snake* was of the serpent looping its namesake with several gigantic coils. It seemed that Captain Hezekiah was to go down like Ahab in *Moby-Dick*. *And good riddance,* I thought.

✦ ✦ ✦

"Well, this is a rum situation and no mistake," said Dr. Drake as we stood, dripping, on the shore underneath the cliffs.

"At least we are alive," said Beatrice. "Is this Cornwall?"

"Yes," said Dr. Drake. "We must make our way up to the top of these cliffs at once. St. Austell is not far. We can find an inn there where we can dry out. I shall send a telegraph to Emery so that he can send us some money, since we have lost all of our things. I am devastated that we have lost the dragon dust."

But at that moment, the serpent's tail swung back over the beach, holding the box of dragon dust, which it placed neatly on a rock. Then it disappeared again. Dr. Drake grinned broadly and picked it up.

"At least some things are going our way," he said.

We started up a winding path that led up from the beach to the cliff top. I noticed that the dawn could not be far off. At least climbing warmed me up a little.

"Did Captain Hezekiah know about us?" I asked.

"I don't think he did," said Dr. Drake. "What worries me more is the whereabouts of Ignatius Crook. I would guess that he is still trying to find the right location to call the sea serpent. But if he is anywhere close, he may well have seen the commotion back there."

"Do you think we're safe for now?" asked Beatrice.

Just then, I could have sworn I saw what seemed to be a very small blue dragon fly out from behind a rock above us and then fly back again. It had beady little eyes and looked at us meanly.

"I am afraid not," said a loud, harsh voice. A large, roughly dressed man carrying a nasty-looking cudgel suddenly stepped out from behind a rock, barring our way. As he did so, he flipped open his coat for a moment, so that we could clearly see that he was carrying a pistol.

Another man, who was also carrying a stout cudgel, stepped out behind us. After looking around to make sure we were really alone, the first man calmly took out his pistol and pointed it at Dr. Drake.

At that, the man we had seen in the pub doorway opposite Dr. Drake's shop calmly stepped from his hiding place and smiled at us. The small, wicked-looking dragon was sitting on his shoulder like a parrot, baring its teeth.

"My dear Dr. Drake," he said, "this is a nice surprise."

"What do you want, Ignatius?" said Dr. Drake.

"You know what I want," said Ignatius Crook. "Just don't do anything ill advised. I think I'll take that." And he reached out and took the box of dragon dust from Dr. Drake.

"You're a beast!" said Beatrice, glaring at him.

At that, Ignatius reached up and prodded his pet dragon, which leapt from his shoulder, made a beeline for Beatrice, and gave her a nasty nip on the arm.

"Hey!" she called.

"Perhaps that will teach you that children should be seen

and not heard?" said Ignatius. "See if he's got anything else useful, would you?"

One of the men grinned and began searching Dr. Drake's dripping pockets. But all they contained were a watch, which did not seem to be working, a pencil, a compass, some loose coins, and a small whistle in the shape of a dragon's head.

"Give that to me," said Ignatius.

"Why?" said the man. "I found it."

"I wouldn't blow on it if I were you," said Dr. Drake as the man held it aloft. Then he put it to his lips and blew out a shrill note that reminded me of the sound Scorcher made after Dr. Drake had fed him. It was obviously a dragon whistle.

"I said give it to me, you fool," said Ignatius.

He glanced up at the sky, took the whistle, and put it in his own pocket.

"Tie them up," he said.

After the men tied us up, Ignatius led us up the cliff path. We soon found ourselves among the ruins of some old towers and open pits. I had read about Cornwall in my encyclopaedia and guessed this must be the site of a tin mine. Above one of the pits was a mining crane with a rope attached to a winch.

"Are you sure this is going to work?" asked the man with the pistol. He was still pointing it at Dr. Drake. "I'd rather just bump them all on the head and then push them into a pit."

"I'm not paying you to ask questions," said Ignatius "I'm

paying you to do what I say and keep quiet. That pit is a bucca hole. I even found a rhyme about it in your diary, Doctor. It goes:

> *Drop them in one by one,*
> *And one by one they'll go.*
> *A good feed's what the bucca needs,*
> *And they will do just so!"*

As Ignatius sang the rhyme, a savage gleam lit up in his eye. When he had finished, the man said, "Well, I don't like it, but you're the boss. You're quite sure there's something down there? I wouldn't want them to be able to identify us."

"Oh, yes," said Ignatius. "Listen!"

And he picked up a pebble and tossed it into the hole.

After a moment a series of loud, angry noises, like a cross between the grunt of a dragon and the thudding of a huge hammer, came out of the hole. They were going to throw us in *there*? Now I was shivering with fear.

"Can't you hear the bucca knocking?" said Ignatius.

"What's a bucca?" asked Beatrice.

"Oh, it is a type of dragon, my dear," said Ignatius. "And not a very nice type. Not like Flitz here." He paused and stroked his pet, which grunted contentedly. "Dr. Drake has told you all about dragons, hasn't he? Big wings, huge claws, sharp teeth, terrible flames. These ones live in tin mines. But I won't say too much about them. That would spoil the surprise. You are going to meet one very soon indeed."

"But we haven't done anything to hurt you," I said.

"That's very nice of you," said Ignatius. "Throw them in!"

The men attached the ropes binding our hands to another rope, which they fastened onto the crane. Then, using the winch, they pulled us up.

"Ow!" said Beatrice.

"Help!" I shouted. But there was no one else about.

"Surely you will listen to reason?" said Dr. Drake as we swung perilously above the gaping pit.

Ignatius smiled.

He swept at the rope with a knife. It cut through. And we fell headlong into the bucca hole.

We landed in a heap at the bottom. I was on top of Dr. Drake, and Beatrice was on top of me. It was so dark I couldn't see much, but I was sure that I heard something large hastening away into the darkness.

"Is everyone all right?" said Beatrice after a while.

"Well—ah—I think I'm all right," whispered Dr. Drake. He was out of breath. He had landed rather heavily to break our fall.

"Where is the bucca?" I asked.

I had expected to see a lot of skulls and bones from the previous victims, but in the dark all I could see was a vague sheen of ore running along the stone walls and a few fish bones. Dr. Drake managed to cut through the rope by rubbing it on a sharp piece of stone he had landed on, and we slowly began to disentangle ourselves and get up.

"Shh!" said Dr. Drake. "Not quite so loud. We don't want Ignatius to hear us. I am afraid that it seems that he doesn't know very much about buccas."

"How is that?" asked Beatrice.

"Well, it's typical of him really. I expect that all he has done is found out that there is a legend about a terrible, man-eating bucca in this hole, and decided that it is all true. He never did manage to separate dragon legend from dragon science. And he obviously hasn't bothered to find out the full facts in my diary."

"So there is no bucca, then?" I asked.

"Oh, yes, there is certainly a bucca," said Dr. Drake. "It's just not dangerous—that's all. In fact, buccas are extremely timid. A bucca makes that knocking sound when it is trying to escape. But Ignatius is right about one thing—the bucca is a type of dragon. Most legends cast them in the role of some kind of goblin or fairy."

"So how do we get out?" asked Beatrice.

"Well," said Dr. Drake, "first we have to convince Ignatius and his hired ruffians that we are not coming out. So I want you to scream and shout as though you are being attacked by a bucca, then go absolutely quiet."

Even though we were in a pretty grim situation, both

Beatrice and I had to do our utmost to stop ourselves from laughing out loud as we howled and screamed and generally tried to sound as though we were being eaten alive by a bucca. Dr. Drake joined in, and so did the poor, frightened bucca itself, which set up a terrible roaring and knocking. After a while, we stopped, but the knocking from the frightened bucca continued.

"Now," whispered Dr. Drake, "I hope that sounded convincing enough. You both died beautifully. But we must find our way out."

"How do we do that?" I asked.

"Didn't I teach you anything at all at Castle Drake?" he said. "I might not always be around when there are dragons about."

I looked round the hole. Now that my eyes had adjusted to the dim light, I could see that the floor was covered in fish bones. There were also some very clear tracks that seemed as though they disappeared straight into the wall.

"There!" said Beatrice, pointing at them.

"Good," said Dr. Drake. "Now follow them."

"But . . ." I began.

"Just follow them," he said.

Beatrice and I followed the tracks up to the wall. Beatrice touched it, and it crumbled away at once, revealing a passage that must have once been one of the old mine workings. The knocking sound grew louder.

"It's an old bucca trick," said Dr. Drake. "They try to hide by covering up the entrance to their hole. But they are too stupid to wipe away their tracks."

We squeezed into the low passageway and crawled along it until we came to a fork. I began heading down the left-hand passage, away from the knocking sound, but Dr. Drake pulled me back.

"Let's follow the bucca," he said.

And so we crawled up the other passageway, which soon opened up enough so that we could stand up. There was a shaft above our heads that was too high to reach, but it let in some light. We followed the passage as it gradually rose up and up. The knocking sound grew louder and louder until suddenly we came upon the bucca itself.

It took one look at us with a pair of enormous eyes and turned in panic to the sheer wall at the end of the passage. In some ways, the bucca did not seem very different from Weasel, except that it was of a sandy colour with a shorter tail and had a large bony projection on the top of its head, which it was using to dig into the wall. That was where the knocking sound had been coming from. Suddenly, it broke through the wall at the end of the tunnel and disappeared in a shower of sand and dirt. As it did so, light flooded in.

"Well," said Dr. Drake, "this may not be the time to say it, but you are extremely privileged. I do not know of anyone else alive who has ever gotten that close to a bucca before. When we get back, I shall expect a full report. But now we must leave this place by the door the bucca has made. Keep quiet until I can be sure the coast is clear."

So, after a short, sandy crawl, we found ourselves back near the ruins of the tin mine. Dr. Drake went ahead of us, then he came back to report that there was now no sign of Ignatius or the other ruffians.

"There is only one thing that puzzles me," said Dr. Drake, gazing up at the sky.

"What is that?" I asked.

"My dragon whistle did not seem to work," he said.

"Are we sure?" asked Beatrice, pointing to some large tracks right next to the hole that Ignatius had thrown us into.

It was only a few miles into the town of St. Austell. Dr. Drake immediately checked us into some rooms in a hotel and set off to send a telegram to Emery. He came back with a fresh change of clothes for each of us.

"We must get to Bodmin as soon as possible," he said. "We shall stay here tonight, for you two need to eat, rest, and get thoroughly dried out, so I have arranged for a coach to take us there first thing in the morning."

CHAPTER NINETEEN
BODMIN

Dragonology is a secret science. Have a reputation
for being a dragonologist and it is very likely your
reputation will be ruined.
—— DR. DRAKE'S DRAGON DIARY, MAY 1851

The town of Bodmin is said to have been founded a great
many years ago by a Cornish saint named Petroc.
According to Dr. Drake, Saint Petroc, who was also the
founder of Padstow—or Petroc's Stowe, as it was originally
known—was one of the earliest dragonologists to live in this
country. One legend tells of him banishing a fearsome dragon
named Tregeagle and another tells of his great kindness to a
dragon with a splinter in its eye. Until recent times, water
from a well in the grounds of Saint Petroc's church was said
to have the power of curing all sorts of eye complaints and, of
course, Saint Petroc's healing chalice was listed among the
twelve treasures of the Secret and Ancient Society.

As we set off through the town, Dr. Drake said, "I'm sure
I don't need to mention that we must be very careful here

not to run into Ignatius or Alexandra or, indeed, both of them."

"But why would Ignatius come here?" I asked.

"There is every reason to suppose that Ignatius has found the clue about Ebenezer's grave in my diary. Although I failed to understand the clue, I'm guessing that he and Alexandra will at least come here to check it out."

"Where is the grave?" I asked.

"It is in Saint Petroc's churchyard," said Dr. Drake. "We are going there now."

When we arrived, the churchyard was empty except for a gardener who was working in the far corner. We went in and began to search around for a gravestone bearing the name Ebenezer Crook. Although we must have looked over every gravestone at least twice, there did not seem to be any sign of his at all.

"I am quite sure that he was buried in this churchyard," said Dr. Drake.

Beatrice and I went to ask the gardener if he knew where Ebenezer Crook was buried. He was tending a grave that did not yet seem to have a stone.

"Are you relatives?" he asked. "For if not, I must ask you why you are interested in Mr. Crook. And if you are, then I must ask you to prepare yourselves for a shock."

"We are the children of two of his friends from London," Beatrice explained, waving Dr. Drake over.

"There has been a terrible business here," said gardener,

shaking his head. "I know some people in this town did not like Ebenezer Crook, and many liked his son Ignatius even less. They said that Ebenezer had strange interests not fit for Bodmin folk. There were a number of people who said that the words on his gravestone were more than a little strange. The truth of it is that his son returned to the town yesterday and his father's gravestone was stolen last night. What is worse is that there was a fire at his house. It was completely destroyed, and now there is no sign of young Mr. Crook anywhere. It would seem that he must have perished in the blaze, although there is no sign of a body. That is strange, too."

"Are the police investigating the matter?" asked Dr. Drake.

"I should say so," said the man. "They are going round the town now. I expect you will be able to prove where you were last night?" And he raised his eyebrows.

"Indeed," said Dr. Drake. "We have just arrived from St. Austell. But can you tell me which one was his grave?"

"It is this very one I am trying to tidy up here," said the man.

"Thank you," said Dr. Drake. "I don't suppose you remember the words that were on his gravestone?"

"I don't, I'm afraid," said the gardener. "There is one person who might be able to help. Mr. Patterson, the local stonemason, cut the words into the stone. If anyone could remember them, it would be him."

He told us how to find Mr. Patterson's house.

As we left the graveyard, Beatrice said, "Do you think Ignatius took the stone?"

"It certainly seems likely," said Dr. Drake.

"And what about his father's house?" I asked.

"Much as I would love to go and look at it, I don't think we're going to find anything there apart from a lot of policemen."

"Do you think Ignatius would have survived, then?"

"If they have not found a body, then I think it is very likely."

When we arrived at Mr. Patterson's workshop, we found that he too was out, but his wife, who offered us some tea and sandwiches, was able to help us.

"It's a strange business," she said. "No one round here liked Ignatius Crook much. He owed people money, and he had a nasty, bullying way about him. But the theft of the gravestone and the burning of his father's house coupled with his sudden appearance and disappearance have given people a lot to talk about. Old Mrs. Hopkins said that she thought she saw streaks of fire coming from the sky just before the house burnt down. But she says all sorts of things. Perhaps it was a warning. Or perhaps Ignatius really did have some kind of—communion—with strange beasts."

"It certainly seems strange," said Dr. Drake. "We only arrived here today to pay our respects to Ebenezer. He had other friends too. We might like to raise some money to replace his gravestone."

"Well, you have come to the right place," said Mrs. Patterson.

"We are a little worried that some people thought the wording on his stone a trifle irregular," said Dr. Drake. "We would like to consider replacing the stone with a similar wording, but we cannot find out what that was."

"Well, it was a long time ago—almost ten years—but there was something unusual about those words, as I recall. In fact, I think my husband may even have kept a note of them. He usually does. Please let me to go and search for them while you drink your tea."

Ten minutes later, the woman returned with a sheet of paper, which she handed to Dr. Drake. "Here," she said. "I knew there was something unusual about it. Apart from the name, Ebenezer Crook, and the dates, 1799 to 1875, there was just this poem. And there's a misspelling, you'll see. He must mean *worms*." Beatrice and I strained to look at it over his shoulder and read:

DR. EBENEZER CROOK
S.A.S.D.
A Child of Bodmin
1799–1875

Brave did I live and bravely die;
Earth holds no secrets here.

Nigh every man shall come to wyrms
Who seeks to persevere.

Yet seeking here is all in vain—
Vain, but still not wrong,
In me you see the thing you seek,
Sought far, so fair, so strong.

"I see what you mean," said Dr. Drake as he handed back the piece of paper. "I think that we may go for something more simple."

He handed back his empty teacup as well. "Please let your husband know that we will be in touch," he said as he ushered us to the door. "Unless the police find the original stone and arrest the villains who stole it."

And we set off up the road.

"Did you manage to decipher anything?" I asked.

"Not now," said Dr. Drake with a smile. "We must find our way to the railway station. It is just outside of town. I think it is time to return to London."

As we waited at the station, Dr. Drake took out a new notebook he had bought and, on a clean page, copied down the words on the stone from memory.

"Beatrice," said Dr. Drake, "you were the one who guessed that Ebenezer took a secret with him to his grave. Try reading this and see what you make of it."

She and I both stared at the verses. I knew she would be keen to beat me to the answer. She wrinkled her brow as she concentrated. Then suddenly, she relaxed and smiled.

"Of course!" she said. "Didn't people used to write codes using the first letter of each line?"

"The first letters?" I said, "Why that's B-E-N-W Y-V-I-S. Is that a place in Wales?"

"No," said Beatrice, laughing. "It doesn't say that. Daniel, do you remember when we were very young? Mother and Father took us to Scotland. We stayed in a hotel near Inverness, at a place called Dingwall. Father had some business up there, I think, and we had a grand time. You were only four and you nearly got bitten by a snake."

"Yes," I said. "I just about remember it. It took us a long time to get there because of a problem with the trains."

"Well, do you remember the mountain Father climbed nearby? We stayed at the bottom and had a picnic. There was Little Wyvis . . ."

"Of course! And Ben Wyvis. If you climb up it on a clear day, you can see all the way to Ben Nevis! And that's where I was nearly bitten. But it wasn't a very bad bite, luckily."

"No, but Mother was quite upset. She said something about us being too young to go on expeditions."

"And it was the year after that that Father got ill, and we started boarding school two years later," I said. "Are we going to Ben Wyvis, Dr. Drake?"

"We are indeed," he said. "But first we must return to London and go back to my shop. I need to speak to Emery. And then we shall take a trip to the Highlands. There is something that puzzles me about this answer, though."

"What is that?" I asked.

"Well, I know Ben Wyvis pretty well. It is the mountain where Scorcher's mother, Scramasax, lives. I know her very well. She was the dragon that was guarding Saint Gilbert's horn. But I am worried about what Ignatius may do now that he has both the horn and the dragon dust, and so I am going back to London to pick up a certain piece of equipment. But it is strange, because I am absolutely sure that the Dragon's Eye will not be there."

"Do you think Ignatius will actually use the horn to tame a large dragon?" asked Beatrice.

"With Alexandra's help, I am sure of it," said Dr. Drake. "And I wouldn't be at all surprised if he used it on the dragon that was summoned by my whistle. If his first attempts were unsuccessful, that would certainly explain why his father's house has now burnt down."

Suddenly Dr. Drake looked up.

"We are being spied on," he said.

"Where?" asked Beatrice.

"There," he said, pointing to a tall tree on the other side of the track.

It was Flitz. He screeched mischievously and then took

off from the branch he had been sitting on, swooping low over our heads before disappearing in a blue flash over the top of Bodmin Station.

We arrived in London early the next morning. As we walked up Wyvern Way, I saw that there was a man standing outside Dr. Drake's Dragonalia as if guarding the entrance. As we got closer, I realised that it was Emery. He gave me a conspiratorial smile as Dr. Drake whisked us straight through the shop front and down the stairs, barely stopping to greet Mr. Flyte, who was serving behind the counter. Dr. Drake led us down the short corridor at the bottom of the stairs and smiled as he opened a pair of double doors and ushered us into a room that seemed far too grand to be in the basement of an ordinary shop. There were several other doors round the room, a marble floor, and in the centre, a magnificent golden statue of a dragon in flight. It was a room that belonged somewhere else entirely.

"Welcome again," said Dr. Drake as he gestured round him, "to Dr. Drake's Dragonalia. Or as I should call it, the London headquarters of the Secret and Ancient Society of Dragonologists!"

"My goodness!" I exclaimed. "How old is this place?"

"The headquarters of the Society is more than six hundred years old," said Dr. Drake. "The shop upstairs is merely a disguise to fool those whose interest in dragons proves superficial. There is much here that I would very much like to show you, but now is unfortunately not the best time for a tour. I must just pick up one or two things in preparation for our trip."

And with that, he led us into another room that was full of trunks and boxes, along with a row of what looked like dragon masks on a shelf.

Although he searched furiously, he could not find what he was looking for. And he was just scratching his head when Emery came in. Dr. Drake explained to him everything that had happened. Then he asked, "Why isn't my flameproof cloak here?"

"I am afraid that Mr. Tibbs paid us a visit last night," said Emery. "Along with Lord Chiddingfold. The police had told the Minister about the fire at Ebenezer Crook's house. He believes that things are 'getting out of control' and that it is Mr. Tibbs, rather than yourself, who should be sent to track down Ignatius."

"Mr. Tibbs?" exclaimed Dr. Drake. "And how would *he* track down Ignatius?"

"I have no idea," said Emery. "The trouble is that Mr. Tibbs demanded your flameproof cloak. He also took a lot of other things. He and Lord Chiddingfold are worried that you might make things worse if you try to go after Ignatius. They wanted to speak to you the minute you got back."

"Then I must go and speak to Lord Chiddingfold immediately," said Dr. Drake.

"I wouldn't do that, Doctor," said Emery. "I think they

are planning to arrest you. 'For your own good,' apparently. And Algernon Green has told the police that you are holding two children against their will. They have been here at least once already. If I were you, I would leave London at once."

In less than half an hour, we had left Dr. Drake's Dragonalia and had taken a hansom cab towards Euston Station. As soon as we turned out of Wyvern Way towards the Seven Dials, we saw three policemen heading in the opposite direction. But our luck did not seem to last. As we reached New Oxford Street, another cab that had been going in the opposite direction, turned round and started to follow us.

Dr. Drake leaned his head out of the window and called to our driver, "I'll give you half a crown if you can manage to lose that cab."

"Very good, sir," said the cabby.

He shook the reins and our cab set off at a brisk pace, but so did the cab behind us. We sped past University College and managed to leave the other cab behind as we turned into Euston Road.

"Who was that?" I wondered as we reached Euston and hurried into the station.

"I don't know," said Dr. Drake. "Wait here, while I go to purchase our tickets."

But as we waited, what should we see but the same cab pulling up outside the station doors? Whoever was inside must have guessed where we were going. We were just about to make ourselves scarce when a familiar voice cried, "Hang on! We've got something for you!"

It was Billy. He and Alicia came dashing out of the cab towards us, carrying a parcel. They looked almost as furtive as we did, and we all shook hands conspiratorially.

"I heard you were coming back to London," said Billy. "Couldn't let you go without wishing you good luck. We spotted you just as we were turning into Wyvern Way, but you sprinted off."

"We thought you might be Ignatius or someone," said Beatrice.

"Not likely," said Billy. "Anyway, we brought you something."

He handed us the parcel.

"What is it?" I asked.

"Oh, you'll see," he said. "Alicia managed to get it. I think she's taken all that stuff about girls being quick to heart. You've ruined her."

But he was smiling.

Beatrice grinned, too. Alicia blushed, but looked pleased.

"Good for you," said Beatrice. "We'll have to tell you about our adventures later."

"They're not over yet," I added. "And I hope you two don't get into trouble over this."

"Oh," said Alicia, "I'm afraid we will. But there is one more thing we can do for you."

It was then that I noticed that rather a lot of policemen had suddenly come into the station.

"They are probably looking for you," said Billy. "But Alicia has a plan. See you later."

Billy winked, and he and Alicia then headed over to a policeman. Billy deliberately bumped into the policeman and said, "Oh no! Beatrice! Run!"

"Quick, Daniel!" cried Alicia.

Billy and Alicia then ran headlong out of the station and back to their cab, which took off at full speed. The policeman, clearly thinking that these must be the two children they were looking for, started after them, shouting, "It's those two children who are in cahoots with that Drake fellow! Stop them!"

Which was just as well. For as I turned round to look for Dr. Drake, I saw that another policeman had been on the very point of placing his hand on my shoulder.

CHAPTER TWENTY
SCOTLAND

It is possible to deal with most cases of dragon attack
using a combination of quick thinking
and energetic running.
—— DR. DRAKE'S DRAGON DIARY, OCTOBER 1851

Nearly everyone has heard of the famous train known as
the *Flying Scotsman,* which leaves Platform 10 at
King's Cross Station in London at ten o'clock every morning and travels from London to Edinburgh in ten and a half
hours. It is nearly quicker than flying. However, Dr. Drake
had said that the route onwards from Edinburgh to Inverness
would have been too slow. He had therefore opted to travel
by a more direct route, which led from Euston, where the
train to Inverness leaves at five minutes to nine in the morning, stopping at Carlisle and Perth before arriving at its final
destination at ten o'clock at night.

Dr. Drake arrived with our tickets and a trolley for our
luggage. We walked along the platform until we came to

our carriage, which was near the front of the train. Just as we were about to get on board, I noticed that the policemen had come out onto the platform.

"They must have caught up with Billy and Alicia," said Beatrice. "I hope that they are all right."

"They brought us this," I said to Dr. Drake, pointing at the parcel.

"Ah," he said. "I wondered where that had come from."

Two policemen were beginning to walk along our platform.

"This is Uncle Algernon's doing," said Beatrice. "They are looking for us."

We quickly boarded the train just as the guard began blowing his whistle and the doors were slammed shut, leaving the policemen on the platform.

We found our seats and placed our luggage in the overhead racks as the train began to pull out of the station. Soon, it was chugging out of the smoky atmosphere of London and into the countryside.

Now that we could relax, we told Dr. Drake about Billy and Alicia.

"I wonder what's in the parcel," I said.

"There's only one way to find out," said Beatrice.

She tore it open. Inside was Dr. Drake's flameproof cloak.

"Excellent," said Dr. Drake. "By the way, when we were at the S.A.S.D. headquarters, I just had time to pick up a couple of books for you both to help pass the time."

He opened his case and took out two thick volumes.

"Remember," he said, "while dragonology may seem very exciting, you will never get very far with it unless you have a grasp of quite a number of other sciences: physics, geography, chemistry, mythology. They are all useful fields of study for the budding dragonologist."

He gave one book to each of us. Mine was an Elizabethan natural history book by a man named Edward Topsell. It was called *The History of Four-footed Beasts*. It was full of rather fantastical illustrations of all sorts of animals—both real ones and others that I had always considered imaginary. Dr. Drake told me to make notes on anything I found that was obviously incorrect. I thought this would keep me busy for quite a while, since just by thumbing through the pages, I saw plenty of things that seemed wrong, such as a story that giraffes were a sort of cross between camels and wild pigs and an idea that hippopotamuses—or hippopotami—were savage carnivores who love to eat meat even more than crocodiles do.

Beatrice's book was a guide to rearing tropical snakes and lizards from the egg. She didn't look quite as happy with her choice as I felt with mine, until Dr. Drake said that he wanted her to read it from the point of view of a person who has been given a dragon's egg to hatch.

"The information isn't exactly suitable for dragons, but it will get you thinking along the right lines," he said.

By around seven o'clock, I grew tired of making notes about things that seemed incorrect in Edward Topsell's book and took to gazing out of the windows. We had left Perth and were speeding through the Scottish Highlands. There were lochs with ruined castles on their shores and mountains covered with purple heather. It was a beautiful summer's evening, and I could see for a long way.

I searched the horizon. In the distance, I saw what looked like an eagle swooping up over one of the mountains ahead. It hovered in the air, and I wondered what it was hunting. But as it came closer and closer, I realised that it wasn't an eagle at all. Its wings were too large, and they were ribbed like an umbrella. It had a long tail with an arrowhead at the end. It had four legs. Its huge horned head turned directly to look at the train. I gasped. It was a European dragon. It wasn't red, like Scorcher. Instead it was green and it was fully grown. It must have been about fifty feet long, and it was flying straight towards the train!

"Dr. Drake!" I cried, excitedly pointing out the dragon.

The creature was now nearly upon us, sweeping round towards the back of the train, almost as though it meant to attack it directly. It was a spectacular sight, but it made my heart pulsate with fear. The dragon swooped so low that its wing tips nearly touched the ground, then it slowed down, flying right alongside the train, its snaky bulk clearly visible through the carriage windows. I watched as it sniffed in great breaths of air and looked into each of the windows with its great eyes. Wisps of smoke streamed back from its nostrils as it flew.

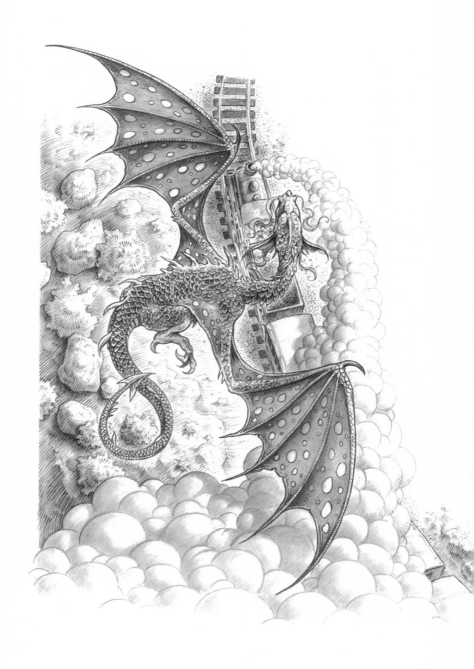

"It's looking for someone!" cried Dr. Drake.

Beatrice and I looked at him in amazement.

"I am a dolt!" he exclaimed. "Ignatius must have sent it after the train in order to attack us!"

"Duck!" he cried as the dragon approached our carriage. But just at that moment, someone must have pulled the emergency handle. The brakes began screeching and the dragon disappeared behind us as we tumbled over and over. When we got up again, the train had stopped and I saw Dr. Drake grab the flameproof cloak.

"Stay here!" he commanded. "And stay down!"

He disappeared.

I went over to the door to close it behind him but I could not resist looking out to see where either Dr. Drake or the dragon had gone.

Suddenly I found myself being pushed back by the same ruffians who had attacked us in Cornwall.

"Help!" I cried. "Leave us alone!"

"Got you!" cried one of the men as he sprang into the carriage and grabbed hold of Beatrice.

I kicked the other man in the shins, and he let me go, but only for long enough to let me see that he was still carrying his pistol. Then the two villains dragged us off the train and marched us across a patch of grass towards a road. A moment later, a black carriage appeared. There was a crate lashed to the back. The two men bundled us inside, and we found ourselves facing Ignatius Crook, who was absentmindedly stroking Flitz and gazing intently at something out the window. Next to him sat the same pale-skinned woman in the black cape and riding boots that I had seen in St. Leonard's Forest. Flitz turned and hissed at us like a cat, his forked tongue flicking in and out as he watched us.

"Let go of us!" shouted Beatrice, trying to move as far away from Flitz as possible.

Ignatius turned to look at us. His white face and teeth were thrown into relief by the gloom of the carriage interior. He tapped on the floor with his dragon-headed cane, and the carriage set off along the road.

"I'm so glad you could make the show," he said. "It is a tragedy, of course. You are just in time for the climax."

He pulled down the carriage window and gestured towards the train with his cane. Most of the passengers seemed to be either cowering in the carriages or running away in various directions. But there was one figure who was standing right near the front of the train, standing stock still and waving his hands high in the air, trying to attract the dragon's attention. It was Dr. Drake. But if he was trying to distract the dragon's attention away from the other passengers, he did not seem to be having much luck, as it was still flying up and down the train. Suddenly the dragon spotted him. It turned and, jetting out a huge spout of flame, bore straight down on him.

Both Beatrice and I shouted frantically, but it was no good. Dr. Drake managed to duck the first jet of flame the dragon blew at him, but then it landed right in front of him, and knocked him flying with a blow from a gigantic claw. As Dr. Drake struggled to his feet, the dragon reached its head back, took in a deep breath, and blew another enormous jet of flame at him. We watched the angry dragon blow blast after blast of searing fire over him until the carriage turned a corner and we could see no more.

Ignatius Crook pushed up the window of the carriage.

"An appropriate end, don't you think?" he said. "For a man who infects even children with his nonsense about conserving and protecting dragons?"

Beatrice and I were too stunned to reply. Ignatius continued.

"No doubt you are aware that I had hoped poor Ernest's end would come sooner rather than later, but needs must."

"You're a monster!" I shouted angrily.

Flitz looked up expectantly, but Ignatius ignored him.

"Oh, I'm worse than that," said Ignatius with a sneer.

"Let us go!" shouted Beatrice. "What have we got to do with any of this anyway?"

"Ha!" said Ignatius. "As though you know anything about how that so-called doctor has usurped my rightful place as head of the Secret and Ancient Society of Dragonologists? You may know that my father, Ebenezer, was not at all disposed to pass on the secret of the whereabouts of the Dragon's Eye to Dr. Drake. But he was a weak man. At the end he repented, and caused a vital clue to its whereabouts to be cut onto his gravestone. But one of you must have spotted the clue, of course? It was in the dragon diary. The Dragon's Eye shall be mine soon enough. I am taking you to Ben Wyvis. The dragon who lives there will no doubt be quite ready to believe that it was Dr. Drake who stole Scorcher when I return him to her. And if she does not, then I have a very simple backup plan."

At this Ignatius pointed at something under the seat. It was the box of dragon dust.

"In any case, I have something to sweeten the bargain," he added. "She is sure to give up the Dragon's Eye when I present her with the two children of the man who stole something else that was very precious to her. And then there will be no one standing between me and the mastery of the S.A.S.D.!"

"Dr. Drake said you tried to poison Father when he wouldn't let you copy the diary," said Beatrice.

"Oh, did he now? That wasn't very nice of him. But I am no friend of your parents. They chose to side with Dr. Drake—may he *not* rest in peace—in preventing me coming into my rightful inheritance, and I shall make sure they suffer the consequences of those actions. But I haven't introduced you to my friend Miss Gorynytchka. She is a friendly Russian dragonologist who has been helping me to reclaim what is rightfully mine. She is conducting some experiments relating to dragon illnesses. I find the topic quite boring myself, but Miss Gorynytchka has achieved some remarkable results over the years, particularly among the nagas of northern India. I believe she has something rather special planned for your parents."

Alexandra Gorynytchka smiled. "I am delighted to make your acquaintance at last," she said. "I was watching you in the forest. At the time I was planning to kidnap you, but after your first little outing with that Darcy boy, I'm afraid you were too well guarded and so I missed my chance. You both seem to have a considerable talent for dragonology. What a shame you will never get a chance to develop it."

CHAPTER TWENTY-ONE
BEN WYVIS

Pity the poor fool who stands between an angry
mother dragon and her beloved chick.
—— DR. DRAKE'S DRAGON DIARY, DECEMBER 1851

The next day, after an uncomfortable night in a dingy
cottage near Dingwall, we set off for Ben Wyvis.

Beatrice and I struggled along, tied together with a rope
held by Ignatius. Meanwhile, the two ruffians were trying to
manhandle a large crate onto a wheelbarrow. Angry chirp-
ing noises were coming from inside and, at one stage, one of
them was bitten on the hand. Alexandra Gorynytchka had
not joined us.

"Scorcher must be waking up!" said Ignatius, stopping to
take a pinch of powder from the box of dragon dust, then
blow it into the crate. "There. That will send him to sleep
again no doubt. But we must make haste. We do not want
Scramasax to catch us on the hillside."

We set off again, but not towards the summit of the Ben. Instead, we skirted it and stumbled along a slope that was covered with shingle and loose boulders. From time to time Flitz flew on ahead, then returned to perch on Ignatius's shoulder. Finally, we arrived under a rocky outcrop to find the mouth of a cave.

By now, Ignatius's hired ruffians were lagging farther and farther behind, and so he made us wait while they dragged the wheelbarrow up the last steep bit and pulled it into the entrance to the cave. Then he lit a torch.

"Bring Scorcher," he said as he led us inside.

It was not a wide cave, of the sort that I had always associated with dragons, but more of a tunnel entrance. There was evidence of dragon activity, however. The roof of the tunnel was blackened with smoke, and the floor was littered with animal bones. Ignatius was soon tugging us along behind him, farther and farther into the tunnel. A smell that reminded me of Scorcher grew stronger and stronger, and it was getting hotter. The light from Ignatius's torch was not very strong, but even so I could see some oddly shaped letters scratched onto the side wall of the tunnel, and the skull and crossed bones of a deer arranged on the floor, almost like a warning. Flitz did not seem to like the place at all. He crawled off Ignatius's shoulder and hid himself inside his jacket.

"We are here," said Ignatius, reaching out his torch into a vast cavern.

I heard the beast breathing before I could see anything.

Then I saw two enormous eyes glaring at us in the darkness. The eyes seemed very angry. But for a brief moment, as they turned towards the crate, they were full of longing.

Suddenly Beatrice gasped. I tore my eyes from Scramasax and saw that the whole floor of the cavern was covered in golden artefacts, with gems sparkling here and there. It was the dragon's treasure. And sitting on the very top of the treasure, her tongue flicking in and out and a thin column of smoke rising from her mouth, was Scramasax.

I glanced at Ignatius. He looked anxious. His eyes scanned the treasure. I guessed he was looking for the Dragon's Eye.

Ignatius bowed and forced us both to our knees.

Then Scramasax opened her mouth and spoke. Her voice was strong and rich, with an accent that was quite foreign, as though she was communicating in a language that was not her own.

"Ignatius Crook," she said, "you are forbidden from entering my lair on pain of death."

"I have come to return your chick," said Ignatius in a quivering voice. "And I have a gift for you."

Ignatius went over to the crate and pulled a latch. Little Scorcher emerged from his cage, looking drowsy from the effects of the dragon dust. Scramasax made a deep rumbling sound, then reached out with her tail and gently lifted Scorcher up. She soothed him, then put him down behind her and stared at us again.

"Now," said Ignatius, "you have your baby back. Stolen by a man I am sure you know: Dr. Ernest Drake."

"Ah, yes. Dr. Drake," hissed Scramasax. "Perhaps he is not the one in whom dragons may place their trust, after all? A human who can help dragons in their hour of need?"

"I fear he is not," said Ignatius, "since he is dead."

"That is a shame," said Scramasax. "We placed a great deal of trust in him. The Society of Dragons was convinced he was the one who could help us. There was a feeling that the world needed a new Dragon Master. Perhaps we were mistaken."

"Ebenezer Crook did not ask you to pass that title on to Drake."

"And he did not see fit to ask us to pass it on to you, either," said Scramasax. "Perhaps he knew what our answer would have been."

"My family has been Dragon Masters for nearly three hundred years," said Ignatius. "If you give me the treasures that Ebenezer returned to you, then *I* would be able to help you. You would have no more trouble from Dr. Drake or his friends, I can assure you."

"No more trouble would be welcome," said Scramasax. "But who are these human chicks? Why have you brought them to me?"

"They are my gift to you, O Scramasax," said Ignatius. "They are the children of the one who stole the treasure that was entrusted to you."

"Indeed?" said Scramasax, her eyes flaming as she peered at us. "That theft made me angry. Dragons cannot control their rage. I grew destructive on that occasion. Many humans suffered for it, and I hid in my cave for a long time afterwards. Where is their parent now?"

Beatrice could not longer contain herself.

"Our father did not steal anything," she said. "It was Ignat—"

But at that Ignatius yanked the rope that held us so hard that we both fell over.

Beatrice got up.

"It was Ignatius Crook," she repeated. "He stole your treasure."

The dragon turned to her.

"Have you proof?"

"Of course she doesn't have proof," said Ignatius. "She is desperate to save her own skin. I can assure you that their parents are the real criminals. They are far away. But they will be punished; I promise you. When I have the treasures."

"Would you bargain with me?" hissed Scramasax. "As I told you the last time you came to my home, shortly after the theft of that precious horn, you are forbidden from entering my lair on pain of death."

"I had hoped," said Ignatius, "that my returning your stolen chick would mitigate your rage somewhat and allow you to see that I am your friend."

"Indeed," said Scramasax. "My doubt as to your motives

has prevented me from devouring you on the spot. But you have returned my chick. I will hear what you have to say outside!"

And so we made our way back out of the tunnel and onto the hillside, followed by Scramasax, who uncoiled her great bulk and slithered along behind us.

I could not believe what I saw when we got back outside. Dr. Drake was waiting for us.

As Ignatius stood open-mouthed, Beatrice and I both tugged at the rope, which fell out of his hands as we ran to Dr. Drake.

"I saw you killed!" cried Ignatius. "You could never have survived so much dragon fire!"

"Ignatius, Ignatius," said Dr. Drake patiently, untying the rope from round our hands. "Even you must have heard of that simple but extremely effective tool of the field dragonologist—the flameproof cloak. What else would I have gone to pick up in London? After you thought I was dead, I made my way here and told Scramasax what you were up to. She wanted to make an end of you right then and there. Luckily, she gave me the time to explain that there were two children with you who were under my care. She agreed to wait just a little longer before getting Scorcher back. It took all my powers of persuasion, I must admit, and it was a pretty close-run thing. Now, I fear, it is you who are in danger. And I rather fear that you will not be finding out where the Dragon's Eye is kept."

"Isn't it here?" asked Ignatius, looking shaken.

"Here?" responded Scramasax. "By no means. But I know where it is kept, so you must pass by me before reaching it. The oldest and wisest dragon in these islands guards the Dragon's Eye, not a youth like myself. I am a mere one hundred eighty years old. Now, I am just beginning—just beginning, mind—to feel myself getting angry. I would start to run if I were you. I would run all the way to the horn that *you* stole from me and bring it here right away."

"Don't believe Drake!" cried Ignatius. "John Cook took the horn."

Scramasax reared back her head and let out a deafening roar. Flames erupted from her mouth, and she shook her head from side to side. Even Dr. Drake began to look a little alarmed, but Scramasax looked at Ignatius again.

"Fool!" she said. "I knew that it was you as soon as I smelt you again."

"Why did you not kill me at once, then?"

"If I killed you on the spot, I might never recover the horn."

"Then I rather fear that it is you who are the fool," said Ignatius. And he laughed. "Saint Gilbert's horn gave me a power you do not know!"

He took out Dr. Drake's dragon whistle and blew three short blasts.

Almost immediately, there was a roar, and the gigantic green dragon I had seen attacking the train swooped down from a crag. It was nearly twice as big as Scramasax, and I guessed at once that it was the dragon that had been summoned when the man first blew Dr. Drake's dragon whistle in Cornwall. Ignatius pointed to us.

"Idraigir," he cried, "your master commands you! Incinerate them!"

The huge green dragon swooped down and would have blasted us all in a moment, had not Scramasax flown up to protect us.

A mighty battle ensued as the two dragons swooped and flew loops round each other, each trying to burn, lash, and bite the other. Scramasax seemed doomed—the green dragon was so much larger. Soon, Idraigir grabbed Scramasax by the neck, and the two dragons became entangled. Unable to flap their wings, the pair fell to earth, where they continued wrestling and fighting with tooth, claw, and tail in a whirlwind of flame. Scramasax was growing weaker. She would not last very long. Suddenly Scorcher bolted from the cave, racing to his mother's side. But in one swipe from Idraigir's tail, he was knocked aside as the green dragon continued its savage attack.

I turned and saw that Dr. Drake was grappling with Ignatius. One of the ruffians took out his pistol and tried in vain to aim it at Dr. Drake. Even Flitz joined in. He was flying round and round Dr. Drake's head, trying to scratch his eyes. Meanwhile Beatrice was trying to wrestle the box of dragon dust from the other man.

"Give that back!" shouted Beatrice.

I rushed to help Beatrice, dodging a sweep of Idraigir's great tail. The man elbowed me viciously in the ribs, but I managed to hold on to him long enough for Beatrice to grab the box he was holding.

"Leave those brats!" shouted Ignatius. "We can deal with them later."

Dr. Drake was still struggling with Ignatius and the man with the gun. Dr. Drake had taken hold of the pistol, which was aimed at his face, and was trying to turn it away. But Ignatius was biting his arm. It could only be a matter of time.

The other man left us and ran over to help them.

Meanwhile Beatrice was opening the box of dragon dust.

"What are you doing?" I said. "We need to get away from here!"

"We have to do something," she said. "Look!"

She opened the box, and I saw that it contained a fine silvery powder and a silver dish.

"Abramelin's Taming Spell!" I cried. "Can you remember the words?"

"I think so," she said. "Can you?"

"Yes, but do you think it will work? Will one taming spell cancel out another? And don't we need three troy ounces? How much is that?"

"I don't know, but we must give it a try."

We stood side by side, and poured out a good portion of dragon dust onto the silver tray and then cast it over the dragons as we cried,

"Ivàhsi yüduin!
Enimôr taym inspelz!
Boyar ugôner gedit!"

Nothing seemed to happen for a moment, then, suddenly, the dragons froze. The green dragon dropped its head and looked about as though it was dazed. Then, seeing us, it came over and looked at us inquisitively, as though asking us what we wanted. The red dragon did not stir. Flitz dropped out of the sky and landed with a bump.

"Save Dr. Drake!" commanded Beatrice.

At once Idraigir flicked his tail and sent Ignatius and his ruffians flying. Dr. Drake lay panting on the ground as the pistol spun away. With a look of contempt, Idraigir trod on it with his huge claw, crushing the barrel flat.

"Idraigir!" cried Ignatius. "Your master commands you! Kill Dr. Drake."

Idraigir looked at him blankly.

Beatrice turned to Ignatius, a look of fierce hatred on her face. Then she relaxed. A dark thought had passed.

"Ignatius Crook," she said, "if I were you, I would leave. Now."

Ignatius stood for a second, open-mouthed. Then he turned and ran down the mountain as fast as he could, followed by the two ruffians.

We went over to Dr. Drake and helped him to his feet.

"Thank you," he said. "You both acted like true dragonologists."

"What about the dragons?" I asked.

"You have charmed them," he said. "You must release them."

"Can't you do it?" I said.

"I cannot," said Dr. Drake. "They are under your command."

"How do we release them?" asked Beatrice.

"It's simple," said Dr. Drake. "You have used only just enough dragon dust to counter the charm Ignatius used. The effect will wear off soon. Until then, I suggest that you simply command them to obey no one but themselves."

I looked at the dragons. A thought occurred to me. Idraigir was a remarkable creature. Who knew how far he could fly? Our parents might be in desperate danger at any moment. I imagined myself riding him triumphantly across the Thar Desert to save them, blasting dark dragonologists from my path.

"But can't we—?"

"No," said Dr. Drake. "This is the most important lesson of all. A dragonologist does not take advantage of dragons, and he never uses spells and charms against them. A dragonologist simply seeks to study dragons and to conserve and protect those dragons that still remain."

I hung my head. But Beatrice came and put her arm round my shoulder.

"Let's do it together," she said.

So we both stood before the three dragons.

"Dragons," said Beatrice, "you are free."

"Obey no one," I added, "but yourselves."

Dr. Drake smiled.

Idraigir let out a sigh.

Flitz sat up and hissed at us. Then he flew off after Ignatius, giving me a nasty scratch as he passed.

"Idraigir," said Dr. Drake, "I apologise that you have had to suffer the indignity of taming, and so crudely. In a way, it is partly my fault, because I did not realise just how much Ignatius had managed to learn or how much help he had gathered. I ask only that you forgive us and that you go in peace."

The dragon bowed his mighty head. He gestured towards Scramasax with his claw. Scorcher, who was not really hurt, was snuffling at his mother, making very sad little noises.

Dr. Drake was at the red dragon's side in a moment. As Dr. Drake knelt by her enormous head, the prone dragon let out a long, rasping breath. My heart leapt, for it seemed that Scramasax was not dead after all. She raised her head a little off the ground.

"Drake," she said, "I am badly wounded. I must sleep in

my lair for a long time in order to recover my strength. Scorcher will be all right. He can stay with me and help me recover, but I have another egg that has not hatched yet. I cannot look after it while I heal. I would not even trust another dragon with it. But you will become Dragon Master, I am sure. So I will trust you. Will you take care of it for me, until I am strong enough to come and claim my baby from you?"

"I will," said Dr. Drake. "And I will keep it safe from harm and raise it properly as a wild dragon, so that when you are able to, you may bring it back to its home here."

"Then I thank you," said Scramasax. "And now I shall tell you what you seek to know. The Dragon's Eye is guarded by the most ancient dragon still living in the British Isles. She is the one who knows the ways of humans better than all other dragons. But I am not able to simply tell you where to find her lair. You must pass a riddle test. Listen:

> *Near Wantley's smokestack lies a door*
> *That's hidden by a barren floor.*
> *Oh, do not go the smokestack way,*
> *Or fire and flames shall make you stay.*
> *Go underground, now that you've heard,*
> *And take the Wantley Dam her word."*

And with that, Scramasax began to drag herself into her lair, with Dr. Drake following. Soon he emerged again, carefully cradling something large and round in his flame-proof cloak.

"This cloak will help to keep the egg warm and your fingers cool," he said. "Do not touch the egg itself; it will burn you. Beatrice, will you look after it?"

I opened my mouth to speak, but Dr. Drake gave me a smile and said, "When we reach St. Leonard's Forest, you may look after it together."

He then turned to Idraigir and said, "But now we have a problem. We still need to solve that riddle and find the Dragon's Eye before Ignatius. Idraigir, will you help us?"

"I long to get back to my lair in Wales. For who else but I can protect my hoard? But for releasing me, yes, I will help you," said Idraigir.

"Then we shall fly back to my home, Idraigir."

Dr. Drake turned to us and said, "Prepare yourselves, my dears. For you two are about to have your first ride on a dragon. But you must be careful, for we will be flying bareback!"

CHAPTER TWENTY-TWO
WANTLEY

When flying a dragon with children, do not practice
inverted manoeuvres unless you purposely *want*
them to fall off.

—— DR. DRAKE'S DRAGON DIARY, JANUARY 1852

Idraigir lowered his long neck to the ground. Dr. Drake took the blanket that had covered Scorcher's cage, folded it several times, and placed it over the dragon's shoulders, so that we would be protected as much as possible from the spines on Idraigir's back. He then helped us to climb up. I sat in front of Beatrice, who gripped me tightly about the waist. Then Dr. Drake climbed onto the dragon too, sitting in front of us so he could direct Idraigir. Just then, Scorcher came padding out of the cave mouth to see us off. He made a few screeching noises, and we waved at him.

"Good-bye, Scorcher!" shouted Dr. Drake. "By the time I see you again, perhaps you will have begun to speak a little! Take care of your mother!"

Idraigir stood up slowly, spread out his huge wings, took two or three steps forward, and launched himself off the mountainside and into the sky. He beat his powerful wings to gain height, then turned in a great, slow arc towards the south. I could feel my heart pounding. Far below us, I could see the forests on the slope of Ben Wyvis and farther off, Loch Ness shimmering in the Great Glen. But soon we were past it, winging our way across the Grampian Mountains and crossing the Firth of Forth.

A few hours later, after flying over a great deal of countryside and several towns, Dr. Drake shouted, "See that city below us? That is London! We are nearly home!"

We did not fly directly over London, for there was too much smoke rising up from the thousands and thousands of chimneys, even though it was July. Instead, we flew around it in a large arc until we were above Sussex, where we began our descent. Idraigir began swooping around in a series of circles, getting lower and lower each time, until he must have been only a few hundred feet above the ground.

"Now," cried Dr. Drake, "there is Horsham. I can see the church spire. Bear to the left, and fly out past the farmland and over to the forest."

Idraigir obeyed, and it was not long before we saw Castle Drake nestled amongst the trees.

"Set us down there," cried Dr. Drake.

The dragon made one or two more slow loops and put his feet down on Dr. Drake's front lawn.

We climbed down off Idraigir's back and saw Darcy, Emery, and Mademoiselle Gamay running out of the house to welcome us.

Dr. Drake turned to Idraigir.

"Now," said the dragon, "I shall return home. I do not like to leave it for long. But if you wish me to, I will return. I would not like to see the Dragon's Eye in the hand of that man Ignatius."

"Then return to us in three days' time," said Dr. Drake. "I do not think this riddle will take me long to solve."

Idraigir bowed. Then, without further ado, he took five paces forward, lunged upwards, and flew into the sky.

Next, Dr. Drake spoke to Beatrice, who, carrying the egg, went into the house with Mademoiselle Gamay. He then led Emery, Darcy, and myself to the old coal shed.

"We need to erect some sort of chimney in here," he said. "We have a dragon's egg to hatch and we are going to need ventilation."

Emery nodded, and he and Darcy set off to find some tools.

"Now, Daniel," said Dr. Drake, "I would like both you and Beatrice to work on this riddle. You will need to write it down in your dragonological record books. But I would also like you to spend time writing notes on everything that you have learned on our adventure."

I went back into the house to find Beatrice.

To my horror, I found that Beatrice had built a little fire

in the grate in the drawing room, even though it was summertime, and had placed the egg among the flames.

"What are you doing?" I cried, leaping forward in order to rescue the egg.

"It's all right, Daniel," she replied. "Dr. Drake says that we must keep the egg as warm as possible, so as not to harm the developing chick inside. Emery and Darcy are going to build a proper charcoal nest for it in the coal shed, but until then we need to keep it here."

Later that evening, Dr. Drake called us into his study.

"Have either of you had any ideas on the solution to Scramasax's riddle?" he asked.

Beatrice and I had spent the afternoon making copious notes in our diaries, with breaks to check on the egg. We had talked about the riddle, but it didn't seem as simple as the one on Ebenezer Crook's grave.

"Is there a place called Wantley somewhere?" asked Beatrice.

"That's the trouble," said Dr. Drake. "I have pored over my atlas, and I cannot find Wantley anywhere. I wish I had my dragon diary. You see, there is an amusing rhyme about a dragon from Wantley. It is based on a legend about a dragon that is defeated by a knight in spiked armour who hides at the bottom of a well. It is very frustrating. I can only hope there is a reference to it in one of my books. I have also written a short note to Mr. Flyte at my shop and one to Lord Chiddingfold explaining what has happened. It may be that they can find out some information up in London."

But much as Dr. Drake searched through all the books in his library, he could not crack the puzzle. Darcy meanwhile, took us to see Weasel, and to help look after Jamal, who seemed pleased to see us every time we turned up with a wheelbarrowfull of meat for him. We even tried to play another game of football with him, but he merely crushed the ball beneath his feet. His attempts at flying were growing better by the day, and I knew that before long, Dr. Drake would have to take him home. We also went to check up on the egg, which was now installed on its own little nest in the coal shed. Dr. Drake showed us how to use the bellows in order to bring the charcoal fire up to the right temperature.

It was two days later that help with the riddle finally arrived. Beatrice and I were on our way to visit Jamal when a carriage pulled into the drive of Castle Drake, bearing Billy and Alicia. Dr. Drake came out to greet them immediately.

"I have a message from my father," said Billy. "He says that a researcher he knows at the British Library has confidently identified Wantley. Given what has happened, he wants you to go there as soon as possible. Mr. Tibbs doesn't exactly agree with him, but this time my father overruled him."

"Where is it?" said Dr. Drake.

"The real Wantley is a village called Wharncliffe," said Alicia. "It is not far from Sheffield."

"Wharncliffe!" exclaimed Dr. Drake. "Of course! The knight that killed the dragon in the legend was called More of More Hall. I knew that More Hall lay not too far away on the other side of Sheffield, but I never thought of Wharncliffe. I shall leave tomorrow. Daniel and Beatrice, while I am away, I would like you to bring Billy and Alicia up to date on everything that has happened."

"Aren't we coming with you?" I asked.

"Not this time," said Dr. Drake. "I am afraid that it is too dangerous."

"And what about the rest of the riddle?"

"Well, I'm hoping that part of it can be solved when I arrive. I'm also guessing that the Wantley Dam is another name for the Guardian. As for the 'word' that I must take her, I have an idea what that might be. In any case, at least we are still one jump ahead of Ignatius Crook."

I went outside with my record book and sat on the lawn. It didn't seem fair that Dr. Drake had taken us along on so much of this adventure but was going to leave us out of the most important part. Danger or not, I would have loved to have come face to face with the most ancient dragon in the British Isles. What stories she would be able to tell about days gone by!

I opened my record book to the page where I had written down the riddle. I took out my pencil and wrote:

I circled it over and over again.

Suddenly my record book was yanked out of my hand. I looked up to see a very familiar blue creature flying off with it.

"Flitz!" I shouted.

I got up and ran after him. Flitz flew through the trees, carrying my record book. Little sparks started to come out of his mouth, and I was worried that my book was going to catch fire. Somehow or other, I managed to keep him in my sights as he came to the road.

Alexandra Gorynytchka was waiting, sitting on a large black horse.

"Do be careful, Flitz!" she said with a laugh as Flitz landed on the pommel of her saddle and presented her with the now smoking book.

I stepped forward.

"That book is mine," I said.

But Alexandra just held up her hand as she flicked through the pages. When she came to the page with the riddle, she tore it out, then tossed the book back to me.

"Here you are, Daniel," she said. "I am glad that you are such a thorough little dragonologist. Luckily for you, I am in quite a hurry. Flitz can be rather nasty when I want him to be."

"I thought Flitz belonged to Ignatius," I cried.

"So does Ignatius," said Alexandra, laughing. "What a fool!"

I backed away.

Alexandra laughed even harder.

"By the way," she said, "I heard a rumour that Ignatius has sent those two ruffians of his here. And this time they won't be taking you prisoner."

She cantered away, chuckling to herself, as Flitz flew round and round her head.

I ran back to the house as fast as I could, and dreading what Dr. Drake was going to say, I knocked on the door of his study.

CHAPTER TWENTY-THREE
THE DRAGON'S EYE

Was it conceited of Elizabethan dragonologist
Dr. Dee to spend so many hours gazing into the
Dragon's Eye? It only reflected himself, after all.
—— DR. DRAKE'S DRAGON DIARY, MAY 1852

The next day, the green dragon returned to Castle
Drake—not a moment too soon as far as Dr. Drake
was concerned—and we set off on our second dragon flight.
Given what I had told everyone about Alexandra and Flitz,
Dr. Drake had decided to take us with him after all.

"It is a question of the frying pan or the fire, I am afraid,"
he had said. "And I would rather have you two with me."

I felt that it had been my fault that Alexandra—and no
doubt Ignatius, too—had discovered the location of the
Dragon's Eye. But Dr. Drake had told me that I could not
possibly have expected Flitz to have stolen my record book
so spectacularly.

"And there is still a good chance that we shall get there
first," he said.

We flew up over Sussex in fine weather. This time we were not riding bareback. Billy and Alicia had brought a fine dragon saddle with them from London, which Dr. Drake said had been crafted by a very discreet saddler indeed. Even so, the journey was not particularly enjoyable this time, mainly because Idraigir was flying at full speed in an effort to reach Wharncliffe as quickly as possible.

Several hours later, we could see the smoke rising over a city that must have been Sheffield. Below us lay a moor.

"That must be Ramsley Moor," said Dr. Drake. "Land there. Wharncliffe lies just to the east of it."

Idraigir began swooping down in circles again and set us down near a small group of standing stones.

We climbed off his back, and Dr. Drake loosened the harness on the saddle.

Then he bowed low. "Idraigir," he said, "I shall not forget what you have done for us."

Idraigir thumped his front feet on the ground.

"Defeat that man Ignatius," he said. "That is all I ask."

Then he took off again and flew upwards. Soon he had become no more than a tiny green speck in the sky.

"Now," said Dr. Drake, "we must search for something that could be called the smokestack. I imagine that it will be some sort of pile of rocks."

But although we searched the moor for several hours, we could find nothing that Dr. Drake thought might be the smokestack, and since we were growing tired and hungry,

Dr. Drake said that we ought to stop and find somewhere to rest for the night.

"But what about Ignatius?" I cried. "He and Alexandra might arrive here any minute."

"That may be," said Dr. Drake. "But you children need food and rest now, and that is what you are going to have. And I have another reason for visiting Wharncliffe. I think we are on a wild goose chase at the moment. I am going to see if I can find out some information."

And Dr. Drake led us off the moor and to a small inn that lay on the outskirts of Wharncliffe village.

When I woke up the next day, I discovered that Dr. Drake had been up and about since the early morning, buying a spade, some provisions, and some candles, and trying to find out as much as he could about anything that might be called the smokestack out on the moor. He had been in luck. The lady who sold him the provisions had said that her mother often used to speak of it. It was a rocky hole in the ground from which, in olden days, smoke and flames had sometimes been seen. There was a story, that very few people believed these days, that there was a dragon under Ramsley Moor, and it was she who caused the smoke and flames to rise up, almost as from a chimney.

"It was right under our noses all along!" said Dr. Drake.

He led us back to the small circle of stones. And there, about a hundred yards away, I found a depression in the ground that was filled with rocks. I could almost imagine that if you crawled down, you might find yourself in some sort of vertical shaft. And when I leaned over it, I could indeed see that there was a sort of vent going downwards.

"Well done, Daniel," said Dr. Drake. "Now that we have found the smokestack, we must find the entrance. It is hidden by a 'barren floor.' Can you see a patch of ground that has nothing growing on it?"

This time it was Beatrice who found what we were looking for.

"There!" she said, pointing to a bare patch of ground a little farther on from the smokestack.

"Are you sure?" I asked. "There seem to be quite a few bare patches of ground about."

"Look!" she said.

Suddenly it hit me. The other patches of ground were irregular, but *this* patch of ground was a perfect diamond shape.

Dr. Drake smiled.

"It's an obvious sign, really," he said. "I wonder that we missed it before."

The soil was soft, and it came away very easily. I began to dig but, after about half an hour, Dr. Drake took over, and very soon we had excavated a sort of pit. Then Dr. Drake's spade hit solid stone. He grew more excited, and excavated more and more quickly. The shape of some kind of ancient doorway began to emerge. When it was finally uncovered, it was about four feet high and about six feet below the surface of the rest of the ground. It was decorated with a fine carving of strange beasts, and at the top was a strange pyramid symbol with an eye. Around the bottom curled the body of a dragon. The door was made entirely of rock, except for the eyes of the creatures, which were made of gemstones. The creatures in the middle looked as though they were attacking each other: there was an ogre fighting a sort of serpent with a man's head, and an eagle and a phoenix battling it out above them.

"Look," said Dr. Drake, pointing to the pyramid symbol at the top. "This is one of the very oldest and most secret symbols of the dragonological societies the world over. Few know it represents the Dragon's Eye. But I wonder how we can open this door."

He thought for a while. Beatrice, however, was feeling all over the door with her hands.

"I think these gems might press—"

"Stop!" cried Dr. Drake.

Beatrice pulled her hand back from the gem in the eye of the phoenix at the last moment.

Dr. Drake smiled.

"I think I've got it!" he said. "Thank you, Beatrice."

"How?" said Beatrice.

"Tell me the names of those four creatures in the middle."

"Well," said Beatrice, "there's an ogre, something that looks like an eagle, a strange bird that looks like it has flames around it, and a sort of snake creature."

"Isn't that a naga?" I said.

"Indeed it is," said Dr. Drake. "And the other creature is a phoenix. Think of the first letters. What is it we want to do with the door?"

"Um . . . naga, ogre, phoenix, eagle?" I said.

This time it was Beatrice's turn to smile.

"No, Daniel. It's ogre, phoenix, eagle, naga!"

"O-P-E-N. Open!" I said.

Dr. Drake began pressing in the eyes of the four creatures. Each time he did so, there was a click until at last the door swung silently open and a rush of hot air came out. It was hot air that carried a scent I recognised—the unmistakable smell of dragons.

Handing us a candle each, which he lit with some matches, we went in through the doorway. Dr. Drake paused to wedge it shut behind us with his spade.

"Do you think the door was booby-trapped?" asked Beatrice. She was obviously wondering what would have happened had she pressed the gems in the wrong order.

"I am sure of it," said Dr. Drake.

We found ourselves in a low, narrow chamber that soon opened out into a tunnel about six feet high with walls carved all over with twisting serpentine shapes.

We did not have time to study the carvings. Dr. Drake led us on down the tunnel as it took a steep angle that led farther and farther underground.

On and on we went, farther and farther down into the

earth, until at last we stepped out into what seemed to be a vast cavern. The walls were covered in the same dragon-shaped carvings that had lined the tunnel. I was awestruck. I stepped forwards, but Dr. Drake grabbed my shoulder.

"Be careful," he whispered.

Looking down, I could see why. There was a chasm at my feet that seemed to run all the way round the walls of the enormous chamber. In the very centre of the chamber was a platform lit by a dim shaft of light coming from an entrance high above it. *That must be the smokestack,* I thought. The light bounced off a huge hoard of golden treasures vastly bigger than the one possessed by Scramasax. There were cups and weapons and necklaces and gems and many other wonderful things, rising in a great pyramid in the middle. And right on the top was a most magnificent gem, reflecting the light round the cavern in what seemed to be a thousand colours.

"These treasures were gathered together during the time of the last great dragon slaying in these islands," said Dr. Drake. "They were brought here by both dragonologists and dragons. They represent the remains of many hoards. They were brought here until the time comes once again when it will be safe for dragons and humans to live in peace. But I fear that day shall be a very long time in coming."

He pointed at the topmost gem.

"That is the most precious treasure of them all. It is the Dragon's Eye. In recent times, only Ebenezer Crook has ever set eyes on it. The Society of Dragons gives each human

Dragon Master the gem to keep, until the time comes when
the dragons must choose a new Dragon Master."

Even though Dr. Drake had been whispering, at the word
"Dragon Master" a sudden hiss filled the hall, and I saw
that, coiled around the hoard, so big and white that it almost
looked like stone, was a dragon that dwarfed even the
mighty Idraigir. From her massive but relatively small

horns, I could tell that this was a female dragon. She raised her gigantic head slowly and turned her flashing eyes to look in our direction. She was the Guardian, the one whom the riddle spoke of as the Wantley Dam.

"What human speaks of the Dragon's Eye?" asked the Dam, her gaze moving from one to another of us as she flicked out her tongue.

"It is I!" cried Dr. Drake. "With your blessing, and that of the Society of Dragons, I am come to claim the Dragon's Eye. I am sworn to conserve and protect all dragons, wheresoever they may be, so that at last the world may learn to respect the honourable science of dragonology."

"I am old," said the Wantley Dam. "Much older than the normal course of a dragon's life, for I am eight hundred and fifty years from the egg. I have protected this gem from the sight of all human beings save true Dragon Masters for many hundreds of years, only relinquishing it to the ones whom I and my companions thought worthy. Yet the last Dragon Master returned the gem to me, saying that none were fit to be his successor. I regret sometimes being so old. I could tell you of times when humans and dragons were not always at war. I could tell you of times when I was young and this whole land was covered with forests from one end to the other. But now I am old. I was old when I began my guardianship, when I called the first meeting of the Society of Dragons and bestowed the Dragon's Eye upon the first Dragon Master. It is nearly time for me to pass on my duty as Guardian to another. I regret that my flame, which was once so strong, is very nearly exhausted. Otherwise I would have tested you with fire and claw. Such would not trouble a true Dragon Master. He would know how to deal with both. Yet I would still hear the secret word that all Dragon Masters must know. And I would know who these children you have brought with you are."

"I am Ernest Drake," said Dr. Drake. "These children are Daniel and Beatrice Cook. They are the children of two very good friends of mine. I have brought them here because their lives are in danger from one who is no friend to dragons. And I know the words you seek."

"I have heard the name Ernest Drake," said the Dam. "I have often wondered why you did not come to claim the Dragon's Eye before. I have a great empathy for Ebenezer Crook. It is not easy passing on to another a responsibility that one has borne for so long. If you would claim the gem now, speak the secret word. But be warned, if the word you speak is not true, then do not doubt but you shall not leave alive. Tell it to me!"

"It is a simple word," said Drake, "although it took me many years and much research to find it. Ebenezer Crook would not tell it to me, but he gave me numerous hints how I might know what it was in his last days. It is—"

But at that moment, a familiar voice rang clear near the top of the pyramid of treasure, shouting: *"DRACO-RACO-ACODRAC!"*

I looked up in shock to see Ignatius Crook dropping onto the hoard from a rope he had used to climb down the smokestack.

The Wantley Dam hissed and twisted her head up towards him and blew out a long gust, forgetting for a moment that she could no longer breathe fire. But Ignatius was ready and, taking the Dragon's Eye from the top of the pile, he dodged out of the way.

"Drake!" hissed the Dam. "Why have you brought this man? He is no friend to dragons. He may know the words, but he seeks to control us for the sake of power and an inheritance he does not deserve to possess!"

"Beware the Guardian, Crook!" called Dr. Drake.

"What?" cried Ignatius. "Beware this toothless, spent old wyrm?" And he laughed again. "You surprise me, Drake."

And with that, he ducked away from the Guardian. She was trying to bite him, but she was finding it difficult because she was so enormous. Ignatius dodged behind a rock, then ran out and leapt across the chasm, clutching the Dragon's Eye. As he did so, Flitz tumbled from his pocket. The tiny dragon flapped frantically, trying to get as far away as possible from the enraged Guardian.

"You fool, Ignatius," cried Dr. Drake. "Would you kill us all? The Guardian has a greater power than you think."

"And I shall use it!" roared the Guardian.

She lowered her head and began to shake so violently that blocks of stone began to fall from the ceiling. Then a strange sound, like thunder, filled the cavern. It seemed to be coming from the dragon's belly.

Beatrice and I blocked our ears.

Then the dragon reared back her head and roared. I felt the whole earth round me vibrate, and I was sure the whole room would collapse. Beatrice and I clung together, and I could see that even Dr. Drake was gripping onto the wall for support. I could not see Ignatius anywhere.

Suddenly the roaring stopped.

The Wantley Dam looked at us.

"Now none shall escape," she said. "I have used a dragon call that has not been heard for some four hundred years. I have summoned every dragon in Britain to my aid. The first ones will be here within a few minutes. And *then* we shall see about the Dragon's Eye."

The silence in the chamber seemed even louder than the dragon's roar. Nobody moved.

Then I looked in amazement to see Alexandra Gorynytchka standing right next to the Guardian. In her left hand she held a strange amulet covered in runes, and in the right an African spear.

"Beware!" cried Dr. Drake.

But it was too late. Before the Wantley Dam could turn to face her new opponent, Alexandra struck deep with the spear, aiming for a spot just under the dragon's huge belly. A jet of black blood spurted out, and the Guardian groaned, rearing up suddenly and flicking her tail around the chamber, which flushed Ignatius from his hiding place on the other side. The ground shook and shook as the Guardian's death throes grew stronger.

Alexandra began to climb up the rope that lead into the smokestack.

"Help me, Alexandra!" cried Ignatius.

Huge blocks began to fall from the ceiling all around us as the roof and the whole smokestack above it began to collapse.

Alexandra turned.

"Ha!" she said. "You are a fool. You have what you wanted. And I have what I wanted—see?" Clinging on to the rope with one hand, she held out the spear and the amulet for us to see.

"Aren't those two of the treasures?" I shouted.

"They are indeed," said Alexandra. "This is Splatterfax—the war amulet of the Viking Rus. We have long sought our ancient treasure, and now I have found it again. You have kept it from us for eight hundred years. As compensation, I am taking this spear. It belonged to Saint George, I believe. As far as I know it belongs in Africa. But it is the only weapon that is sure to kill any dragon."

"But you promised to get me out!" said Ignatius.

"As I said," said Alexandra with a laugh, "you are a fool. And by the time the first dragons the Wantley Dam has summoned appear, I shall be long gone."

"Flitz," called Ignatius, pointing towards Alexandra. "Attack her!"

Flitz streaked upwards. But when he reached Alexandra, instead of attacking her, he chirped once, looked back down, and then flew up out of the hole.

Alexandra let out a loud cackle as she continued to climb up into the smokestack. When she reached the top, she cut the rope so that it fell back down into the chamber. Then she disappeared.

But by now, the whole ceiling was coming down.

Dr. Drake turned to look at us.

"Get back into the tunnel!" he called as he ran towards Ignatius Crook.

"Come back!" cried Beatrice.

"I cannot," he said. "You cannot imagine how terrible it will be if Ignatius Crook gains this power."

"But what of the other treasures?" I said.

"We can do nothing about them now," said Dr. Drake. "It is the Dragon's Eye that is important at the moment."

As Dr. Drake reached Ignatius, a shower of rocks tumbled down, knocking them both to the floor. The Dragon's Eye flew out of Ignatius's grasp and skidded away, resting right on the edge of the chasm. Dr. Drake made to get up and grab it, but Ignatius picked up a huge rock and hit him on the back of the head so that he went down again. Then, in his rage, he hit him again and again.

"Stop it!" cried Beatrice.

We had been backing into the tunnel, but suddenly I made a decision. I dashed out of the tunnel, dodged a falling boulder, and grabbed the Dragon's Eye.

Ignatius was right behind me. He lifted the rock in his fist, a mad gleam in his eye.

"The Dragon's Eye is mine!" he screamed.

But just as he was about to smash the rock down onto my head, the tail of the dying dragon lashed out, loosening a carved pillar that tottered and fell. Beatrice ran forwards and dragged me back just before the pillar smashed into the ground, making an impassable barrier between Ignatius and us. More rocks began to fall.

"Leave this place!" cried Dr. Drake, getting to his knees. "Take the Dragon's Eye to Emery. He will know what to do!"

Ignatius Crook went over to Dr. Drake and grabbed him. Dr. Drake was weakened from the blows he had taken and could do nothing as Ignatius pulled him towards the lip of the chasm.

"Now," cried Ignatius, "give me the Eye or I will push him over the edge!"

"Get out of here!" cried Dr. Drake. "Do what I tell you!"

"Silence!" shouted Ignatius, pushing Dr. Drake so that he was hanging halfway over the chasm.

"No matter what," said Beatrice, "we cannot let Dr. Drake die."

I agreed.

I went up to the fallen pillar and held out the Dragon's Eye.

"Don't be fools!" called Dr. Drake. "You don't know what you are doing."

"We do," said Beatrice.

I handed the rock to Ignatius, who stretched out his hand to receive it. Dr. Drake scrambled back up onto the ledge.

"Now, Drake," said Ignatius, "you die!"

"No!" wailed Beatrice.

But just as Ignatius was about to reach him, a hail of rocks began to fall, dislodging the pillar that had separated us. Ignatius was knocked clear across the chasm, and we rushed forwards, pulling Dr. Drake back into the mouth of the tunnel. He got to his feet. But instead of going forwards, he went back. Ignatius was frantically trying to dodge the massive blocks that were falling all round him.

"I am sworn to protect all creatures," said Dr. Drake. "Even creatures like Ignatius."

"No, Dr. Drake!" I cried.

But Dr. Drake paid no heed. He went to the chasm and reached over.

"There is still time, Ignatius," he cried. "Jump!"

Ignatius Crook got to his feet and, putting the Dragon's Eye into his pocket, clambered over the Guardian's still-writhing coils, took a running jump, and just managed to catch Dr. Drake by the hand. Dr. Drake had to haul him up, slowly and very painfully. When Ignatius had finally crawled over the edge and stood up, Dr. Drake gestured back towards the tunnel. Now most of the roof had collapsed, and the walls of the chamber were starting to fall in.

"Come, Ignatius!" he shouted. "It is the only way!"

But instead of coming up the tunnel, Ignatius laughed and began to run in the opposite direction, round the rim of the collapsing chamber.

"And let you have the Dragon's Eye, Drake? Never, do you hear? Never!"

And as he disappeared into a cloud of falling rock, masonry, and dust we heard him shout again, "Never!"

We hurried back into the tunnel. Only when Dr. Drake was sure that the rocks had stopped falling did he leave us for a moment.

"Wait here," he said.

He went into the chamber. A few minutes later, there was a strange roar and a sudden flash of light. Beatrice and I both raced back in to find Dr. Drake stumbling towards us.

He smiled sadly.

"The Guardian was not quite dead," he said.

As we left the cave, a mighty roar sounded, very similar to the one that had shaken the cavern to its foundations and summoned the dragons to the Guardian's aid. But it did not last as long.

"She has called off the attack," said Dr. Drake. "It was her dying breath. The dragons were flying here to fight, but now they will come here to grieve. It is a shame that we cannot stay here to see them, but they will need privacy now, so that they can properly lay her to rest."

And as we turned to go back to Wharncliffe, I almost fancied that the sky had darkened in the far distance, as though a huge mass of flying creatures was coming our way.

CHAPTER TWENTY-FOUR
THE DRAGON MASTER

The Dragon Master has the gravest responsibility of
all —— for he must not only learn but also teach.
—— DR. DRAKE'S DRAGON DIARY, JUNE 1852

A few days later, we were back at Dr. Drake's home in
St. Leonard's Forest, sitting in the sun on the pockmarked lawn, watching the rabbits, and occasionally going
to check up on the dragon's egg. We were not feeling very
happy. Uncle Algernon was due to arrive later that afternoon
to take us to his home. The luggage had arrived with a
newspaper clipping, which said there had been several
sightings of dragons recently, even one involving an attack
on a train. The police were taking these reports with the
usual large dose of salt and had put it all down to the unsea-
sonably hot summer weather.

Neither Beatrice nor myself felt like leaving Dr. Drake.
As soon as we had recovered from our ordeal, he had

immediately begun his summer school again. We had also been helping to look after Jamal, taking him round on an enormous leash. When he was trying to fly, it took three of us to hold him down. He had not escaped his compound again. We learned from Billy and Alicia that they had initially been grounded after stealing the flameproof cloak from their father, but that when Lord Chiddingfold had found out what had really been going on, he had relented and sent them back to St. Leonard's Forest. Even Mr. Tibbs had grudgingly admitted that things seemed to have turned out "all right."

Beatrice had been reading up on how to care for baby dragons and was sure that the egg would be hatching in only three weeks or so. And although we didn't know very much about the Dragon's Eye and Dr. Drake refused to talk about it, we felt sad that it must now be buried so deeply in the collapsed cavern that there was no chance of ever getting it out again.

"Surely you are not sorry that Ignatius is dead?" I asked.

"Sorry?" said Dr. Drake. "Yes, I would be sorry, if I were convinced it were true. But I am sure that there was more than one tunnel leading out of that cavern. How else do you suppose Alexandra managed to get in there? And so I will not give up worrying about Ignatius just yet. And another Guardian must be found."

"Even though Ignatius has the gem?" asked Beatrice.

"*If* he has it," said Dr. Drake. "But we are sure of one thing: Alexandra Gorynytchka has stolen at least two of the treasures. Perhaps she even has Saint Gilbert's horn and my dragon diary as well."

"Can we come and see you next summer?" I asked.

"Of course," said Dr. Drake. "But I have a feeling that our real troubles are only just beginning. I'd rather you didn't get mixed up in it." He gave a long pause, and then continued: "But do you know? It is important for me to train as many young dragonologists as I can, especially ones as talented as you. Your parents will be proud. I think that they will talk to your uncle Algernon so that he will not stand in your way again. And I think it will be a real pleasure."

There was a twinkle in his eye.

The twinkle grew brighter when Uncle Algernon arrived. As soon as he did, Dr. Drake left to see about making some tea.

Uncle Algernon took us to one side.

"Good afternoon, Beatrice. Good afternoon, Daniel," he said. "I'm afraid I don't see any point in beating about the bush. I want to ask you a very serious question. I'm afraid I don't agree with it at all, myself, but then, your father and mother are stubborn people. And Dr. Drake has sent them several telegrams through his friend Emery. They would like to know if you would like Dr. Drake to become your tutor full-time."

"What?" cried Beatrice. "And not go back to school?"

"Exactly," said Uncle Algernon. "You see, I told them it was not a good idea, but—"

"But it's a fantastic idea!" I cried. "To stay here and learn about dragons!" At which Uncle Algernon made a face.

"And to help the baby dragon to be born!" cried Beatrice. "And to help Jamal get ready to go home!" And he made an even bigger one.

"But it will not all be learning about dragons," said Dr. Drake as he returned with the tea. "For to know about dragons, you must learn to study and cherish all the other sciences and learn at least two other languages and read an awful lot of books. So you will find that I will work you harder, possibly, than you are going to like, if you are really to learn about dragons."

"We don't care," I said. "We would love to stay. Wouldn't we, Beatrice?"

"Well, yes, I think so," said Beatrice thoughtfully. "But may I ask a question?"

"Of course," said Dr. Drake.

"Will our parents be safe?"

"Your parents will be quite safe," said Dr. Drake. "They are returning on a ship as we speak. I do not think that they are at any risk from Alexandra Gorynytchka and her dragon illnesses for the moment."

"Thank goodness," said Beatrice.

"I hope they tell us about the nagas," I said.

"What on earth is a naga?" asked Uncle Algernon.

"It's a sort of dragon," I said.

At which Uncle Algernon raised his eyes to the sky as though he was the only member of our entire family to have any sense, and said, "Dragons, indeed!"

Later that evening, when Uncle Algernon had left, Dr. Drake called us into his study. It had now been fully repaired. Emery was there too, smiling broadly, as was Mademoiselle Gamay, Darcy, Billy, and Alicia.

"Now that you two are officially to be my full-time pupils," he said, "we shall resume our daily briefing. You may tell me what you have learned, and I shall try to teach you what I know and give you exercises to do. But you must remember that it is only from close observation—of the obvious as well as the less obvious—that you will really learn anything at all. As you have seen, even I sometimes miss things that are right in front of my own nose."

And then he got up and went over to a small chest, which he unlocked with a key.

"Dr. Drake," I said, "there is one thing I do not understand."

"And what is that?" asked Dr. Drake.

"Why wasn't Alexandra interested in the Dragon's Eye?"

"It wasn't important to her," said Dr. Drake. "It is really only a stone, after all, and its power is confined to the British Isles. Alexandra Gorynytchka was mainly interested in recovering Splatterfax. Now that she has it, I am sure that she will return home where, I hope, she will not cause any more trouble. No, I am more worried about Ignatius. Although she fooled him, he is still likely to have my dragon diary, and he will be even more desperate for revenge. But there is one thing I am sure of. He does not have this. Look!"

And he held up the Dragon's Eye.

"But we thought Ignatius had—" began Beatrice.

"Ha!" cried Dr. Drake. "Alexandra was right about one thing. Ignatius is a fool. It was easy enough to pick his pocket! Didn't you notice the flash of light when I went back into the Guardian's chamber? She was not quite dead, remember, and her fire was not quite extinguished. Look into the gem!"

As we looked, a very strange thing happened. For instead of my own reflection, or Beatrice's, all I could see was the reflection of Dr. Drake as though, having captured his likeness, the gem could reflect nothing else.

"The dragons have decided!" he said. "I am to be the next Dragon Master and to bear the great responsibility that comes with this gem. But if dragons and humans are both to survive into the future and to live side by side in peace and harmony, my most important task must be to train the one who will come after me. So the question is: who is to be the next Dragon Master? Who indeed?"

AUTHOR'S NOTE

The existence of remarkable Victorian dragonologist Dr. Ernest Drake first came to light with the alleged discovery of a book simply entitled *Dragonology* in early 2003. This volume, a natural history book with the central theme of dragons, was supposedly the sole survivor of a print run of only one hundred copies. It was particularly interesting in its treatment of dragons as actual, living animals rather than the mythological creatures they had hitherto been supposed to be. The one remaining copy was said to have been found in an old shop near the Seven Dials in London, not far from where Dr. Drake's Dragonalia itself must have stood. *Dragonology* was edited by the current author and published in facsimile form, to some acclaim, in late 2003. Since then, further works by Dr. Drake have come to light and have been similarly published.

The author's diligent researches into Dr. Drake and his life both in London and in St. Leonard's Forest in Sussex have proved as fruitful as they are ongoing. However, rather than simply write Dr. Drake's life in a dry, bibliographical fashion, the author determined to write the story of Dr. Drake and the S.A.S.D. from the point of view of one of the people who came to know him best of all, his dragonological apprentice Daniel Cook. In this way, the author hopes to convey a sense of what it would really have been like to have studied dragons and dragonology with Ernest Drake, in addition to recounting some of the most important events to take place both in the world of the dragons themselves and in the history of the Secret and Ancient Society of Dragonologists.

One thing is certain: as further facts emerge about Dr. Drake and his tireless work conserving and protecting dragons, they are sure to be revealed.

Dugald A. Steer
London, May 2006

Don't miss the book that started it all!

For true believers only, here is the original
volume that introduced the world to
Dr. Ernest Drake and his science of dragonology.

And don't miss these *Dragonology* companions — must-haves for dragonologists everywhere!

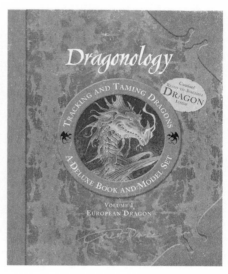

Other books by Dugald A. Steer:
Collect all the 'Ology books!

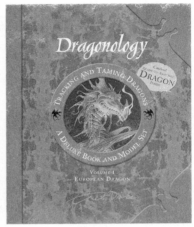

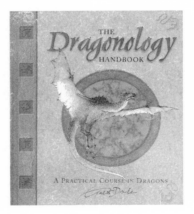

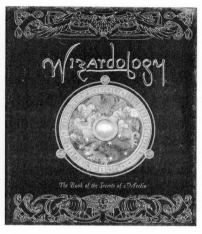

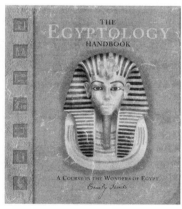

Available *only* from Candlewick Press
wherever books are sold

www.candlewick.com